About the Author

Lexie Winston has been an astronaut, rock star, princess and time traveller. In her dreams. But none of the dreams have lived up to what becoming an author has been like. She gets to live in a world of pure imagination, and her heroines get to do the things she's always wished she could.

When not writing books, Lexie is a mother of two gorgeous teenagers and the wife to a patient and understanding man. They live in Western Australia and are lorded over by a black toy poodle. She loves camping, reading and if her iPad was stolen, her world would explode. (It has the kindle app on it.) And you can find all links at

www.lexiewinston.com

Seductive Sins Collection

(Reverse Harem Series)

Glorious Gluttony

Gangs, Guns, and Glory

Glory Glory Hellelujah

Crowning Glory

What's the Story, Morning Glory?

Galaxy Circus

(Sci-Fi Reverse Harem Series)

Apprentice

Stagehand

Whisperer

Mama - Galaxy Circus Novella

Performer

Ringmaster

Interlude

A Night Most Wicked - Galaxy Circus Novella

Broken Promises

(Dark Poly Romance Series)

Secrets Kept

Lies Untold

Trust Broken

M.I.T.H.O.S

(Contemporary RH)

Spies Like Me

Spies Like Us

Storm View Stories

(Contemporary Standalone RH)

Ice Me Out

CROWNING GLORY

Seductive Sins Series

Book 4

LEXIE WINSTON

First published by Neighpalm Publishing in 2024

Crowning Glory: Seductive Sins Series 4

Mobi format: 978-0-6459663-2-9
Print: 978-0-6459663-3-6
Cover design by Dazed Designs
Editing by Elemental Editing

Chapter One

It's all I can do not to hyperventilate as Lucifer ushers me down the long room to the table at the front. There, he gestures for me to take the seat on his right, and through my panic, I hear Leviathan tell the others to make themselves comfortable. Eventually, Lucifer is the only one standing, and he grabs the glass before him and raises it.

"I can't tell you how thrilled I am that Hell has finally chosen an heir to replace me, and what a powerful choice. I can't wait to see Hell thrive under Gloriana's rule, which will be straight after her crowning ceremony in twenty-four hours."

The crowd bursts into loud, excited chatter once again.

No, Luc, it needs to be a week before the crowning ceremony so Glory can learn all she can from you before you blow this popsicle stand. The voice inside my head sounds exasperated but affectionate, and now that I'm paying more attention, I realize it has a feminine tone. From the way my uncle swears under his breath and wrinkles his nose in annoyance, I can tell that he hears the voice as well.

"Fine," he mutters before throwing his hands up.

"Actually, scratch that, change of plans. We will have the crowning ceremony in five days. That will give my staff enough time to arrange a ceremony fit for a queen." He lowers his voice and mutters, "Five days, and that's it. I will wait no longer to chase down my errant mate who seems to have slipped through my clutches once more."

Fair. The voice sounds amused. The crowd seems to roll with the sudden change of plans like it's a common occurrence, but Luc's annoyance turns to sly amusement.

"And as one of my final declarations, I will be authorizing a change of transportation." The crowd's excited chatter drops. "Please return your Segway to the transportation warehouse located at the portal to Earth. There, you can swap them out for your new mode of transport." He waves a hand, and a hologram appears, hovering above the table. "Hell kangaroos."

"What the fuck?" I mutter as the voice inside my head groans.

Luc, you fucking asshole.

Luc snickers as stunned silence resounds in the room. The picture is of a kangaroo on steroids, and it shows a child climbing into the pouch where their head sticks out as the kangaroo bounces around. It then swaps to another image of a person riding a kangaroo's back, with reins guiding them in a direction and a saddle to hold them in place.

"You have kangaroos that big here in Hell?" I ask my uncle as he finally takes a seat, but it's the voice inside my head that answers.

No, we don't. I am now responsible for creating enough Hell kangaroos for our entire population. What were you thinking? It's crucial to teach Gloriana everything she needs to know, and now I will have to funnel half my power into your infernal idea. The voice is pissed, and Luc winces slightly.

"Sorry, I didn't think about that," he says quietly so only I can hear him.

No, of course you didn't, you never do. You are such a child. I know you have grown bored and tired, but now is not the time for acting out. You better step up to the plate and teach Glory all she needs to know, because I don't doubt the challenges are going to start rolling in at any second, the voice scolds fiercely before falling uncomfortably silent.

"Crap, I may have fucked up," my uncle admits as staff starts pouring out of a doorway to the side, placing plates full of food in front of each of us at the head table before attending to the guests at the other one.

"What the fuck, Luc?" Leviathan demands from

my uncle's other side as soon as the crowd is distracted with their food.

"Yeah, I know, sorry." Luc sounds sheepish as he picks up his cutlery. "I wasn't thinking. I was simultaneously pissed that Kerry escaped us again and thrilled that an heir has been named so I can now chase her down. I got a little lightheaded and giddy." I watch, my eyes wide with shock, as my uncle cuts his meat into small pieces before delicately stabbing it and eating a bite.

I don't have to wait long, though, because he turns to me and beams. "Glory, sweet girl, I should have known you were going to be the Hell heir when you collected three mates, and then three more, and then even my gatekeeper." He leans forward to look at Julian, who is on my other side. "Congratulations, my friend."

Julian nods his head in thanks but stays quiet. I think he knows I'm struggling with everything, and that I'm one small push away from losing my shit.

"What the fuck was all that?" I ask as I finally catch my breath.

"Lucifer is an idiot," Leviathan says affectionately, and I see him pat my uncle's leg under the table while keeping a stern frown on his face as he looks over the attending demons with disdain.

"He's not wrong," my uncle agrees, "but I promise, despite everything, I will spend the next five days giving you a crash course in becoming the ruler of Hell. If you had grown up here, you would have been marked a lot earlier, and we would have had many years to teach you what you need to know. If only your mother hadn't been fooled by that bastard." He clenches his fist and bangs it on the table.

"Ah, well yes, that bastard may be part of the reason we came to Hell," I tell my uncle quietly, and he freezes before turning to me, his green gaze piercing and intimidating. I can see the ruler of Hell now.

"What do you know of Mabuz?" he asks calmly, the atmosphere turning tense and frigid in a second.

"So many things—things that we probably need to talk about in private," I murmur, my gaze going to the demons feasting joyously.

His gaze follows mine, and he gives me a short nod. "Yes, of course. Let's get through this, and we'll make our apologies. They will understand that you have a lot to learn in five days." Luc looks down the table, finally paying attention to the other people seated with us, before turning and looking at Louis, Carter, and Nolan, who are on the other side of Leviathan and Beelzebub.

"You certainly have a well-rounded and gorgeous group of mates, Glory. I can't wait to get to know all of them better. I always wanted nephews. I also can't wait to go to Earth and sample all the wonders it has to offer, see my sister again, and love on my other niece and nephews there." He sounds almost giddy, and his mood changes are giving me whiplash. I'm not sure that it's real. I'm almost certain it's an act designed to keep everyone around him on his toes.

"You can call me Uncle Luc," he tells my mates, who all stare at him with wide-eyed shock, except Julian.

"Like fuck I'm calling you Uncle Luc," he protests.

Luc reaches over and ruffles Julian's long hair, messing it up and grinning affectionately. "Of course not, because I'm like a father to Cerberus. You can call me Papa."

Julian chokes on the mouthful of wine he'd just taken, and red liquid splatters across the black tablecloth. I just shake my head at the craziness that is my uncle. He and my mother are like two peas in a pod, I can see it now.

Luc waves a hand, magically cleaning up the mess Julian made while muttering about messy children. Julian continues to spew obscenities, but I choose to ignore it all. I'm going with the smile and wave attitude for the moment.

I look out across the guests who are all enjoying the feast. Alcohol is flowing, and the food seems to be never ending. Occasionally, a shout rings out, and an argument ensues, but it is quickly subdued by the guards who linger around the far sides of the room—just far enough away to be inconspicuous, but close enough to break up any fights before they become brawls.

Something out of the corner of my eye catches my attention, and I turn to see what it is. In the very first few seats, not far from us, sits a group of people who don't seem to be partying quite as enthusiastically as the rest—two men and a woman, all blond and similar enough to be relatives. The two men just look bored, but the woman is glaring at me like I pissed on her plate before it was served to her. Her gaze keeps flitting to my side and turns lusty for a moment before becoming an annoyed scowl. What is this bitch's problem? I follow her gaze and realize she's making doe eyes at Julian. Ah, great, my first experience with what must be a rejected ex. Instead of asking him, I lean in closer to my uncle.

"Who is the woman right in front with the blond hair?" I ask him, and he frowns, trying to figure out which one I'm talking about. In his defense, there are quite a few with blond hair. "The one who looks like I pissed in her Wheaties," I clarify, and his confusion clears, and he smirks.

"That's Imogen. She's my niece and your cousin, and she has quite the thing for your mate, Julian."

"She's a raving lunatic," Julian mutters from my side before leaning closer and whispering, "Despite her many attempts, I have never touched her, I swear. She tried to convince Luc that an arranged marriage between his bloodline and me would be what Hell needed to declare her the heir. Watch her very carefully."

I hear what he's saying, but I'm more confused about Lucifer's original statement. "Your niece? My cousin? How?" As far as I know, my mother only has one brother, and he's sitting next to me.

"What do you know about the origins of demons?" Luc asks, leaning back in his throne-like chair and setting his piercing green gaze on me. Gone is the manic light, and in its place is a surprising seriousness.

"Nothing, to be honest. Mom would always change the subject whenever I asked."

He smiles sadly. "That doesn't surprise me. Petra always felt shame over her lustier tendencies, which was what was wrong with the whole system in Heaven to start with." He claps his hands and turns his body to face me. "The CliffsNotes version is that the creator created Earth, but he gave man free will and, well, we all know how that went, but he tried to instill all his angels with what is known as the seven heavenly virtues. It really was hubris on his behalf, because there is no such thing as perfection. Angels still had free will, and everything must be in balance. There is no light without dark, and there can be no good without evil."

"So demons are evil?" I ask, not sure I can agree with that, and Luc shakes his head.

"No, of course not. We all started out as angels, but we're angels who evened out the uneven balance, the yin to the angels' yang. War broke out, and the creator despaired. I saw that things would not go well for the less virtuous angels and approached the creator to allow us to leave, to create our own world away from the heavenly plane, and he was so thrilled about the idea, he granted me rulership. He did not like to see his creations fighting."

"So demons really are fallen angels?" I ask, and he shrugs.

"Yes, in a way, except we committed no crimes apart from being imperfect in the eyes of the rest of the creator's flock."

"And your niece?" My gaze flits back to the woman who is now in deep conversation with the two men sitting beside her. Their heads are huddled close, and the conversation looks intense.

"Ah, yes, my niece and her two cousins on her mother's side. You see, angels are still being born, and some are still showing that they lean more toward the sin side than the virtue side. These angels are shipped off to Hell after they've had their wings taken from them. I think it's because Heaven is still so unbalanced. Instead of virtues and sins living in harmony, they kick out the sin inclined angels."

Wings? But I still have questions that are more important. "But wouldn't that also happen here?" Luc shakes his head.

"No, because we don't care if you show kindness or any of the seven virtues. We value balance. Think of all the demons you know. Are any of them evil and completely driven by their sin?"

I shake my head. "No, of course not. We absorb the sins of others to feed ourselves and power our magic."

"Exactly, but the angels couldn't understand that. They think people should be the embodiment of their sin or virtue."

"So your niece and her two cousins are recent imports from heaven?" My gaze goes back to the trio. They've finished whatever conversation they were having and are back to glaring at me.

"Yes. My brother Gabriel is the very embodiment of an angel, and he wouldn't stand for his daughter to be sin inclined, so she was shipped off here. She's been here a couple of years but has never truly fit in. Her arrogance is her downfall."

"And what was her supposed virtue?" I ask as I watch the woman push her chair back and stand up. Big, white wings appear behind her, and the room falls into a sudden and shocking silence.

"Charity," Luc says, leaning back and folding

his arms as he watches his niece with a small amount of amusement.

"So that makes her sin envy," I say under my breath, and he nods. "Shit." I have a feeling I know what's coming.

"Gloriana Luxure, I challenge you to mating rights for Julian Beamus and the claim of Hell's heir."

Chapter Two

"Of course she freaking does," Julian mutters beside me as I just stare at the bitch with wings. "She doesn't care about consent. Mate challenges are stupid, and I have no idea why they are even allowed. What about my wants and needs?"

I cock my head to the side and look at her wings fluttering behind her, feeling kind of envious myself. "Why does she have wings? I thought you said angels lose their wings before they come to Hell."

I gain a small amount of amusement from seeing Imogen's frustration as I fail to give her the reaction she was hoping for. I think she might have been hoping for dramatics. The crowd starts to murmur again.

"Our bloodline is the only one who doesn't lose them." He stands up and looks down at me, his own wings bursting forth behind him, and the crowd gasps with awe. They, too, are a pristine white, but they sparkle with gold and red flecks. "I'm sorry, but Hell's rules are clear, and all challenges must be accepted. I promise I will explain everything to you before you have to face her." He turns to Imogen, a hard look on his face. "Your challenge has been acknowledged and is set for twenty-four hours' time. Gloriana Luxure, do you accept this challenge, or do you concede now?"

"Sure, why not? I have a spare moment tomorrow to kick her ass." I stay relaxed in my chair, waving a casual hand in her direction despite feeling complete and utter panic in my soul, but there is no way I'm going to show any weakness in front of these people.

Good girl, the voice whispers quietly in my head, her approval lessening some of that panic. Surely if she didn't want me to be heir to Hell, she wouldn't have chosen me in the first place. Hopefully I can fulfill the potential she saw in me.

Lucifer nods while Imogen's anger rises at my casual attitude. "Due to your status of septimax prime, you must not seal your bond with your final mate before tomorrow's challenge, or you will risk the life of all seven mates, as this challenge will be to the death," he cautions.

My eyes drift to each of my mates in turn. All seven of them are glaring at Imogen so hard that she would be dead if they could manifest lasers from their eyes.

"I agree," I acknowledge reluctantly.

"And when I win, I'll fuck your last mate next to your cold, lifeless corpse," Imogen announces.

"He really doesn't get a say? That doesn't seem fair," I ask out of the side of my mouth.

Lucifer sighs. "If she wins, it doesn't mean a mate bond will form with her. The embodiment of Hell is not that cruel. It just means that he becomes available to become a mate again, so no, if she were to win, that doesn't mean Julian would be her mate, it just means you were not worthy to keep him as your mate."

You are very worthy to have him as your mate, and I would never break that bond. She will have to kill you to break it because I won't. The voice inside my head sounds furious. *I only break them when the mate is truly unhappy. I admit I sometimes get it wrong—not often, but sometimes."*

That's actually a relief to hear. The guys made it sound like it was a common occurrence.

Challenges often are, but rarely does the challenger win. I make sure of it. The voice sounds smug, and I feel even more relieved it's on my side. *Now say something back. The crowd is getting restless, and you need to appear strong.*

"And when I win, I'm going to tear those pretentious ass wings from your back, set you on fire, and then use them to fan the flames." I take an indolent sip of my wine, acting us unperturbed as I can, like I don't have a single worry in the world.

The crowd is silent once more before bursting into applause and cheers. Yup, I guessed it, nobody likes to be reminded of things they once had. It's worse when they are smug about it, and I bet she does it all the time so she can feed off the envy of people around her.

Luc sits down, and the crowd continues on with their feast like nothing happened.

"Huh, I was kind of expecting a few more challenges, to be honest," I say, and Luc shrugs.

"They might come. The people at this feast are only the ones who are in my inner circle, and as such, they aren't really willing to rock the boat. You were chosen by Hell itself as the heir, and that is good enough for them."

"They are hoping to stay on your good side," Leviathan says from Luc's other side, "so no other challenges will come until they see what happens with the first one."

"You better win. We don't want that harpy in charge of Hell." Beelzebub leans forward and pierces me with a glare. "Can you fight?"

I shrug. "I can hold my own with a human, but I'm not sure with someone like her. Does she have different magic than us?" I'm not sure what angels can do. Demons' magic is limited mostly to conjuring things and greater strength, speed, and senses than humans. Some of us can levitate objects as well, but that's not one of my skills.

"No, angels have the same magic as us. We're essentially the same species, but they start training with swords very early on." Leviathan lowers his voice so it doesn't carry further than the table. "How are you with a sword?"

"Fuck, I'm not sure I could even lift one, let alone fight with it," I admit, and my uncle starts to look concerned.

"It's up to you to choose the terms of the fight now that you have been challenged. That means you decide where and whether weapons are allowed."

"Can we choose any weapon?" I ask, an idea forming inside my brain, but it's something I need to discuss with my mates.

"Yes, or you can rule them out altogether and just go for hand-to-hand combat. You get to decide. Remember her wings will give her an advantage over you, and I can't do anything to stop that," Luc says, sounding annoyed.

But I can, the voice inside my head says. *After all, you are of the original bloodline.* She falls annoyingly silent again, not elaborating on her cryptic comment. I can see my uncle is just as annoyed as I am. He tosses back whatever was in his glass before holding it up for a refill from one of the servers.

Imogen has retaken her seat and is happily eating like she doesn't have a care in the world. The two men on either side of her continue to glare at me and sometimes at Luc, but everyone else has lost interest. My mates continue to portray an air of calm, but I know the minute we are in private, they are going to lose their shit. I wonder what Carter and Louis had to do to control Nolan.

I locked them all into their seats and threatened them with pain worse than death if they said anything, the voice divulges, and my uncle's eyebrows jump at the admission. *They can't get involved, or you will forfeit. I will not have all of my carefully laid plans ruined.*

"If you have been planning this, then why wasn't I aware?" my uncle mutters under his breath, sounding pissed off.

I kept cautioning you for patience and told you that change was coming. It's not my fault if you don't listen, the voice says waspishly.

"You've been saying that for twenty-seven years, so excuse me for not believing you. It was starting to sound like a line." Luc sounds just as pissy as the voice does.

It doesn't matter anymore, but now you need to see to it that my chosen heir does not get defeated by that prissy angel interloper. She's a fucking hypocrite, looking down on other demons while envy courses through her body. She believes that if she can rule Hell, she can have all the demons deny their sins and, in time, they will be allowed to return to heaven. This can't happen. The voice sounds furious. *I will not have my children taken from me.*

"Okay, great, we are all on the same page, so

can we forget this farce of a dinner so I can leave and prepare myself? I'm annoyed at the machinations of this world, and I've only been here less than a few hours. I kind of wish we'd just stayed on Earth and tried to solve our problems there, because I'm not sure that I can win a fight with a sword wielding, winged angel.

If you were crowned, I could imbibe you with the powers of Hell, and there would be nothing she could do that would cause you to fall. Alas, Luc wasn't thinking clearly when he dragged you here before this crowd.

"Listen, you old—" Levi slaps a hand over my uncle's mouth before he can insult the all-powerful Hell energy. "How was I to know you were going to name her heir there and then?" he argues, and the voice inside me sighs.

Sorry, it was unavoidable the minute she crossed the threshold to the room. I should have advised you to have dinner elsewhere. The voice sounds slightly abashed.

"You think? Or, you know, you could have told me that my niece was going to take my place. If we were all on the same page, things wouldn't get missed."

Yes, you are right, but there is nothing we can do now. You have to prepare her to win and teach her how to deal with the politics of Hell.

I feel the presence leave my mind again and finally take a moment to just breathe. I know I can't go on without consuming more food, so I slowly pick at the meal in front of me, tasting nothing while my mind whirls around with everything I've learned. We haven't even gotten to the information about Mabuz yet.

I have a feeling this evening is going to be a long one.

The meal drags on for an indeterminable amount of time. Courses come and go, and the alcohol flows. The guests all seem to enjoy themselves immensely, but the head table is fraught with tension. Every time one of my mates starts to ask a question regarding the challenge, they quickly get shot down, so the table is reduced to small talk. To their credit, Lucifer and his two lieutenants do a good job of keeping that small talk moving, engaging my mates and moving up and down the table. They obviously have experience at keeping up appearances, and I guess the eight of us are going to have to cultivate a public persona if I truly am the heir to Hell. I'm still not sure about any of this, and I'm about to explode with impatience when Luc finally stands up.

"Friends, stay and enjoy the festivities, but it has been a long day, and my niece and her mates are weary, so I will be showing them to their living quarters. I'm sure I don't need to remind you that the private royal wing is off-limits to anyone who's not preapproved." He's staring at his niece when he says this, and I feel my eyebrows jump with surprise. She's not preapproved to live in the royal wing. That's interesting. "An announcement will be made regarding tomorrow's challenge, so keep an eye on your devices and the big screens."

With that declaration, Luc waves his hand, and I feel my body start to shiver, and then it lurches before we find ourselves in a long, tastefully decorated hallway.

"Whoa, you can teleport!" Mason groans, putting out a hand to steady himself as he looks kind of crazy-eyed at my uncle who just smirks.

"Yup." He shrugs and waits for us all to recover from the sudden journey. Only Leviathan and Beelzebub seem to have been unaffected by the transport. I guess if they use it all the time, it's something they are used to, but it's all I can do to stop myself from vomiting everything I've eaten at his feet. It would serve him right, though, especially with no warning.

"Despite the late hour on Earth, it is still midafternoon here. Would you mind if I sent for some tea and coffee, and we had a meeting to exchange all pertinent information? You can tell me everything about Mabuz," Lucifer asks through clenched teeth. "I can also tell you everything you need to know about the mate challenge and being named heir to the kingdom and what being crowned will entail." Lucifer sounds less smug now.

"That sounds like it may be a good idea, but would you mind giving us a moment please? I'm sure my mates would like to lose their shit in private, and I can assure you that letting them get it all out will allow our meeting to go much smoother," I suggest.

"Of course. The far room is our bedroom." He points to the large doors at the end of the hallway. "The room to the right of that is a sitting room. Shall we all meet there in say, an hour?"

"Sounds great, thank you."

"These are your rooms. There is one for each of you, but I'm sure you can sort all of that out." Lucifer winks before waving a hand and taking off with his two lieutenants toward his own room.

"Family meeting?" I ask the group, but I don't get to answer before Nolan sweeps me off my feet and over his shoulder, while Carter opens the door to the closest room. "I guess that's a yes." My words are muffled against his broad back. A hand comes down across my ass, and a sharp, stinging pain makes me yelp with surprise.

"What the hell?" I ask as he places me back on my feet and glares at me, his eyes glowing red with his wrath.

"Heir to Hell?" His tone sounds accusatory, and I don't like it one bit, like it's my fault I've been named heir to Hell.

"Excuse me?" I prop my hands on my hips and glare at him, not intimidated one little bit by his glowing eyes.

"Whoa, hang on, let's all take a deep breath." Teddy steps between us, holding up his hands.

"Yeah, man, don't blame Glory, it's hardly her fault." Ben glares at Nolan, and I feel a rush of warmth for my new mate. I appreciate that he's defending me against Nolan despite the fact that he's huge and intimidating.

"God, Nolan, cool your jets. Why is your first reaction always anger?" Julian throws himself on the bed and wiggles his body until he's comfortable, his eyes drifting closed. "I'm exhausted. Wake me when we make a decision."

Nolan's wrath changes targets, and he sidesteps Teddy and moves toward a sleeping Julian, his hand raised like he wants to strangle him. Louis and Carter jump into action and drag him away.

"Really, it shouldn't have come as any surprise to any of you." Mason holds up a hand, lifting one finger. "One, she's a direct descendant of the original ruler of Hell." He lifts another finger. "Two, she's the first septimax in hundreds of years." Mason lifts a third finger. "And three, she's freaking amazing. Of course she is the obvious choice for the next ruler of Hell. You're going to do amazing, babe." He comes over and hugs me, whispering his congratulations in my ears, and I can't stop myself, I burst into tears.

He pulls back and holds me at arm's length, eyeing me warily. "Oh shit, I think she's broken. Did I break her?"

Chapter Three

Mason looks around the room for help, his eyes filled with panic, and I can't help snorting a sob, which makes things worse.

"Oh my little fiery chicken wing, here now, everything is going to be okay." Louis comes over and takes me from Mason, leading me to a nearby chair in a little sitting area to the side of the bed. He settles himself before dragging me down onto his lap and wrapping his arms around me. My sobbing dies down as I allow his warmth to soak into my body. He's speaking to me in French, and although I don't understand any of it, it's soothing just having him do it.

Carter manhandles Nolan onto the other sofa and nudges him every time he goes to open his mouth. Teddy and Mason join us, sprawling on the floor. Ben looks around, a little unsure, but Carter pats the sofa on the other side of him. "Sit here. Nolan is all bark and no bite."

Ben skips around, patting Carter on the shoulder. "Thanks, but I don't mind a little bite with my bark," he says, winking, and Carter chuckles.

"Good to know." Seeing them kind of flirting should be turning me on, but right now, it's doing nothing, which is how I know that I can't just stick my head in the sand and pretend this hasn't happened.

"I guess now that Glory has been named heir, she won't be able to leave Hell once she's crowned." Teddy rips off the Band-Aid and gets right to the heart of the matter.

"Never mind that. What the hell do I know about ruling an entire nation?" My words are shaky, and Louis gives me another encouraging squeeze. "But yes, I guess that's something that needs to be addressed as well as the mate-slash-heir challenge. What a freaking bitch. She didn't even let me catch my breath before throwing down a challenge."

"I think that was the point," Mason says. "Throwing down a challenge in the hopes of keeping you off-balance and unfocused."

"Not to mention before you sealed your bond with Julian so you can still be killed. That's the only way she can become heir and keep Julian. Once you two seal that bond, she can still become heir, but it means we all die." Ben's teeth worry his lip, and to my surprise, it's Nolan who reaches around Carter and taps his mouth, stopping him from chewing a chunk out of it. Ben's eyes widen with surprise, but he stops chewing on his lip.

"No one is going to die. Glory is a menace in hand-to-hand combat," Nolan reassures Ben. My wrath mate has seemingly recovered from his outburst. He turns to me, then says, "Sorry for shouting. I was shocked, but Mason is right, you are the logical and perfect choice for the next ruler of Hell."

I jump off Louis's lap and throw myself at my first mate, wrapping my arms tightly around his neck. A breath of air gushes out of his mouth when my knee meets his groin by accident, but I don't care at the moment. "Thank you," I whisper to him at the same time as he whispers, "I'm sorry," and wraps his arms around me.

When we pull apart, my tears have completely dried up, but he wipes away the tear tracks from my cheeks.

"Now, we plan," he says, kissing me gently.

Nodding, I climb off his lap and move to sit next to Louis. "Okay, so heir to Hell, all right, okay. I guess the first thing I need to ask is, are all of you willing to stay mated to me, knowing that we have to give up everything on Earth?" I brace myself for their answers. Although I'm almost certain nobody's going anywhere, I can't help but panic a bit.

There is no hesitation as all six of them chorus

their affirmations and reassurances that there is no place they'd rather be.

"Mason and I have nothing keeping us on Earth," Teddy assures me, and Mason nods his agreement.

"Nope. I, for one, am excited to see what ruling Hell entails, and if you don't need us in any capacity, then I'm sure there are plenty of things we can find to occupy our time."

"My club is in capable hands. Your brothers, while young, have good heads on their shoulders. I'm sure they will be fine running it," Carter reasons.

"Tasty Treats is in perfectly capable hands as well. Depending on whether or not you need me from day to day, I may open my own little bakery in town. I would like to stay busy," Louis tells me. I wiggle a little bit, excited to hear he intends to continue baking. Thank the Lord, or maybe Uncle Lucifer.

"And I would like to continue to eat your treats, so it sounds like a win-win situation."

I turn to Nolan who shrugs. "Maybe Kerry's father and I can do a swap. He can run Wrathful Bonds for me for a little while, and I can take over Hell."

"Or here's an idea. Why doesn't Kerry take over Wrathful Bonds? Her father may be just about ready to retire and enjoy time with his wife. Kerry would be perfect for the job." I sit up, a little excited at the idea of helping my friend out.

"And Lucifer and Tweedledee and Tweedledum would enjoy it too." The voice comes from over on the bed. I guess Julian wasn't sleeping too hard, because he's obviously been keeping up with the conversation. He sits up and pushes his hair back from his face, his eyes heavy with sleep.

"That's actually a good idea, and no one is going to fuck with the four of them," Nolan agrees, and I feel my mouth drop open. Whoa, okay. "And now that the girls' mother is out of the picture, there is nothing to stop us from staying here. I would have liked more time to go back and put plans into place, though, because five days doesn't give us much time to get organized."

I hear a rustle and see that Julian is climbing off the bed and coming over to join Mason and Teddy on the floor, but he is carrying one of the pillows under his arm.

"That rule about time spent on Earth and Hell and, really, all the laws are amendable with the start of Glory's rule, so Glory could make it so people can come and go from Earth as often as they want. It would probably be a popular decision. The twice a year thing really chafes a lot of demons." He looks between Teddy and Mason for a moment before grinning and throwing his pillow on the floor, but instead of putting his head on it, he rests his head in Mason's lap and his feet in Teddy's, the pillow completely forgotten.

Mason and Teddy look at each. Mason's mouth drops open in shock, but Teddy just shrugs and puts his hands on Julian's feet, giving them a squeeze and eliciting a moan from my sloth demon. "Ugh, my feet are so sore after running all the way from the portal," he grumbles and flutters his eyelashes at Teddy. "Thank you, big man."

I'm not entirely sure how that works when Cerberus did all the running, but who am I to question the nature of their bond?

"Yeah, but you know what demons are like. If there is reason to cause a stir, then they are down for it," Louis points out, and Ben actually puts his hand up like he wants to answer this question. It's freaking adorable. He looks like a school kid about to burst out of their pants.

"Ben, you don't need to put your hand up," I assure him, and he drops it, blushing slightly.

"Even if you put limits on it, like duration, demons will still be happy with that. I also think maybe buying some demon only hotels and limiting them to only being able to stay in those would also be smart. They would be less likely to cause trouble if they know they are being watched over. Put some heavy penalties in place if they cause problems, and you'll find most of them will stay in line. I'd also suggest a list of approved venues they can attend, like Carter's club or Louis's restaurants—demon run establishments that can run interference if something goes wrong."

I can't help but stare at Ben. His ideas are all smart ideas that really should have been put in place already.

"Wow, you've really thought about this." Julian nods approvingly at my envy mate who nods.

"Yeah, being an illegal made me wish for a lot of things—better options for all demons."

"I'm not sure about finances," I start, and Julian sits up abruptly, scoffing.

"Pfft, the royal coffers are overflowing. Luc hasn't spent money in years. He just comes up with super crazy schemes to keep himself amused. Ben's ideas are excellent, and if we charged a small fee for realm travel, then the coffers would refill in time. We could also employ someone to guard the gate so I don't have to be there twenty-four seven."

"Speaking of which, how often do you need to shift?" I ask, voicing something I've been wanting to know. Are we going to be living with a mouthy, three-headed dog more than Julian?

"About once a week, give or take. Sometimes more often. There's no hard and fast rule now that we are completely in sync."

Well, that's a relief. "So everyone wants to be here? One of my first acts as ruler of Hell isn't going to be dissolving any of our mating bonds?" I say it out loud so that I know for sure we're on the same page, but everyone vehemently disagrees, and that's one less thing to worry about.

"Okay, the mate challenge. Any suggestions?" I ask the group, knowing they have more experience with it. "How attached is Luc to his niece? Is he going to be pissed if I kill her?"

Julian shudders, sinking back down and resting his head in Teddy's lap again. "Fuck no. She's done nothing but cause trouble since she arrived. If, for some reason, she ended up dead, no one will mourn her, not even the two who are always with her. You should hear the way she speaks to them sometimes, like they are nothing but the dirt under her shoe. She really has the angels' superior attitude down pat. It just doesn't fly with demons."

"Okay, so death is on the table." I can't believe I just said that, but I don't want to start my rule with someone gunning for me and my mates. Let's say I win and let her go about her life as normal, then what are the chances she's going to give up her wants and desires? Slim to nada. I'm not going to be the idiot who makes that cliched mistake and end up with all of us dead down the road.

"I suggest you either get really good at using swords really quickly, or we come up with another idea," Julian says flatly, and it's quiet for a moment while my mates think.

"What about a gun? Is that out of the realm of

possibility?" I ask, unsure of the exact challenge etiquette, and my mates exchange glances.

"No, I would say not, but you, as the person challenged, need to declare if weapons can be used. Some specify a certain weapon, so if you say guns, then it means she can use one too, but if you just say weapons, then she probably won't think to bring something else to the fight," Mason says as a smile creeps across his face.

"In fact, I think we should store a whole arsenal in your interdimensional space, and you can take your pick on the day. I say go with heavy firepower. Demons are more resilient than humans, and a nine millimeter might not cut it."

"And what, just whip it out and shoot her the moment the fight starts? Sounds like cheating to me." I have no idea if any of this is going to fly.

"Actually, the demons would respect the shit out of you. Finishing the fight within seconds of it starting shows you mean business." Nolan rubs the stubble on his chin. He looks tired and drawn, and I know the stress is getting to him. He needs to go blow off some steam. In fact, when I look around, the whole group looks exhausted.

"Nolan's right, and Mason's idea definitely has merit," Julian agrees, but Ben is shaking his head.

"I only just taught her how to make one. She needs to practice between now and the challenge to get good at opening it within seconds, not to mention her space is empty, and we will need to fill it."

"Pfft, don't worry about it. Teddy and I can key her to both of ours, and she'll find exactly what she needs in either of those," Mason reassures Ben.

"You know how to?" I ask my pride mate, surprised since he didn't grow up in Hell.

"Yeah, Mason taught me when we first started seeing one another. My father's death broke something inside my mother, and she was never the same, and my grandmother was human. My mother was the result of an affair with a demon. Her father would visit often enough to teach her about being a demon, but he never stuck around for long, and eventually, she just ignored that side of herself, though her work for the MC certainly fed her pride, but I never really saw her use her magic. I'm pretty sure it's because she didn't want to slip up in front of Kenneth. It's probably the only smart thing she ever did."

"Okay, so after my meeting with Lucifer, I need to work on my quick draw skill, so to speak."

"Your meeting. Don't you think we should all come along?" Carter asks, and I shake my head.

"No, I need all of you to be at the top of your game, so while I go to my meeting, you guys do what you need to do to top off your sins. Fuck, fight, flirt, feed, whatever you need, but when the challenge happens tomorrow, I want everyone to be on the same page." My eyes narrow on Julian before swinging to Nolan. "And you two need to sort out your shit. There are eight of us in this relationship, and I can't be the person pulling all the emotional weight, especially because I will have a country to run, not to mention two little girls whose lives are about to completely change." I lay down the law, and I think both of them see how serious I am, because neither of them argue with me, but Julian's eyes glimmer with excitement. I have a feeling that he's going to goad Nolan into an angry fuck, and while I would love to be there, I have important information to talk to Luc about. Carter will make sure they don't kill each other, and Louis will make sure that Carter doesn't get too swept along with the lust. It's nice to have teamwork.

"I think I should probably come with you so I can talk to Luc about Matius's soul," Mason says quietly, and Ben nods as Teddy reaches over and gives Mason's leg a squeeze.

"Me too. I might know things that he needs to know."

"Okay, so you three come with me then, while those four go and stock up on energy, and then once we're done, you can help me practice creating my interdimensional space so it happens as quickly as you can all do it." Hell knows I need all the help I can get.

"Glory, do you want to be the heir to Hell?"

This question comes from Ben, and I stare at him with shock.

"You mean I have a choice? I thought it was a done thing," I ask, looking from mate to mate before settling on Julian, who would be the most knowledgeable—I hope.

He frowns and shakes his head. "I'm not certain, but I think once Hell selects an heir, that's it, and I'm almost certain Lucifer would hold you down and place the crown on your head before quickly ditching you. He's done his time, and he's over it. Look at his latest announcement. Pretty soon, the demons are going to rise up and over-throw him if there are too many more decisions like that."

I wait for the voice inside my head to chime in, but it's been silent since we left dinner. Do I want to rule Hell? Well, it was certainly never one of my goals in life, but when I think about declining and returning to our previous life, there's something inside me that screams no, like this is where I'm meant to be, and although it's scary and certainly going to be something different, I want to succeed. I also want to help Luc. It's time he got a chance to live, so if that means it's my turn to step up and take responsibility, then I'm strangely okay with it.

"Yeah, actually, I do. I think we're going to rock this shit—eventually. I look at it as a new challenge, and having all of you by my side will make it that much better."

A wave of relief rushes through me as I admit this out loud, and I think it goes a long way in reassuring my mates. Sure, we still have a lot to figure out, but knowing we are all on the same page is a big step.

Chapter Four

Exactly an hour after Luc gave us time for a family meeting, Teddy, Mason, Ben, and I are being shown into the sitting area by a guard who was standing just outside the room. Luc looks up as we enter, and an honest and welcoming smile stretches across his face.

"Welcome. I wasn't sure if you were still here or bolted for the portal the moment my back was turned." I can hear the insecurity in his voice, but I appreciate the fact that he let us make the decision instead of locking us in a room and not letting us escape. It goes a long way in earning our trust.

"No, we're here and ready to accept the enormous responsibility that was thrust upon us," I say a little wryly as I take my seat, and he nods.

"Yes, I can imagine it was quite a shock. It was one I wasn't expecting either, but I am happy with the choice. I have been waiting many long years for an heir to be chosen. I hope I can do as much as possible to make the transition easy for you."

Luc is no longer wearing the tailored suit he was at dinner. He has on jeans and a shirt and is bare foot. Leviathan and Beelzebub are still wearing their uniforms, which look like black combat fatigues with a symbol on the upper right chest. I tried to get a look at it earlier but wasn't able to make it out. All three of them have a glass of wine on the coffee table in front of them, and they are relaxing on a large, circular sofa, which is big enough for a football team.

"I hope everything went alright with your mates." He frowns with concern as he looks over my shoulder like he's expecting the others to join us.

"Yes, I think we are okay. I brought these three because they may have information about Mabuz that you need. The other four are sorting out their… differences." I think that's a polite way to put they are getting their shit together. "I need them all on the same page, so they are working out any animosity they still have, and then they are going to take care of their needs."

Luc nods, the frown dropping. "That makes sense. The only way forward is united and harmonious, and I think you're smart to insist that they work out their petty grievances. I know how infuriating Julian can be, but I think he was dreadfully hurt when Nolan left."

"Yes, my mates are idiots who don't know how to use their words. We are working on that," I confirm, and the three with me give me a put upon look, which I ignore. "So how about we tell you everything we know about Mabuz, and then you can tell me what I need to know about the mate-slash-heir challenge?"

"Sounds like a plan."

We spend the next forty minutes filling Lucifer and his two lieutenants in on everything we have learned about Mabuz. Ben takes most of the lead, but Mason chimes in about his ex who is locked in the Fabergé egg. He even produces it for Lucifer to study.

The room is silent as he spins the egg around and then holds it up to his ear before returning it to the stand on the coffee table.

"Yes. Your ex's soul is in there. I can sense it, but I'm afraid without the book of spells Mabuz convinced Petra to steal from me, I can do nothing to release him."

Mason grunts and nods, but I can see the frustration in his eyes. "How did Mabuz even learn of the book?"

"Mabuz used to be as close to me as these two are," Luc begins, and I grimace, thinking that he and my mother shared a lover.

Levi chuckles. "Not like that, Glory. Get your head out of the gutter. He was our platonic friend."

"Not that he didn't try," Beelzebub says dryly, and Luc rolls his eyes.

"No, Mabuz was that friend who was always trying to improve his own situation. He was never happy with what he had, and he wanted more. I didn't feel for him the way I felt about Levi and Beezle. We knew we were all mates for many years, but we kept it behind closed doors, mostly because I didn't want them to be targeted for who they are. Mabuz found out about them being my mates and felt like he was betrayed."

Levi scoffs. "What an asshole. No one can control where a mate bond forms."

"To get back at me, he decided to romance my sister. I also think that was when his delusions of grandeur became a reality."

Beelzebub takes over the explanation. "Because he was in Luc's inner circle, he knew about the book of blood magic. We always caught him looking at it with more interest than was warranted for a book that was kept behind spelled glass."

"Where did the book come from?" Teddy asks, and it's something I've been dying to know. "And why didn't you use it?"

Luc smiles. "Despite what people think of me, I'm not as crazy and as indulgent as I seem. The book was gifted to me by the Hell entity, and I was told to be wise with it. When I read the majority of the spells, I was horrified to discover most of them were fairly destructive and evil, and I decided then and there that I wouldn't use any of them."

"You were being tested." Mason nods his head, his eyes widening with realization. "Demons could have actually become as evil as angels are pious."

"Yes, exactly. Instead, I chose one or two that would benefit the demon race as a whole and shunned the rest, but Mabuz couldn't understand that. He thought I should at least know the spells myself, but some of them were downright nasty. I didn't need to trap souls or make demons my slaves to have power, let alone human sacrifice. Hell bestowed all the power I needed to rule upon me, so I locked the book away under spelled glass. In hindsight, I should have just thrown it into Mount Doom and gotten rid of it."

"I told you so," Leviathan mutters, but Luc ignores him.

"Then he seduced Petra. She was the only other person with the right blood to break the spell I cast over it. She had always felt a huge amount of shame because her sin was lust. Our brother made her feel worthless, and she was always trying to please men. Of course Mabuz betrayed her. I was so angry, I said some harsh things, things I didn't mean in the heat of the moment, and she fled to Earth where I wasn't able to speak to her. I was so glad to hear that she met her mates there. From what I know of your fathers' families, they are good men. I only hope that, one day, I can see her again and beg for her forgiveness for my harsh words."

I reach over and pat my uncle's knee. "I know she feels the same way, but she does have a stubborn streak, and she was worried that if she returned to Hell that she would be named heir." Luc shudders, and Leviathan and Beelzebub cough and splutter before trying to hide it.

"While I adore my sister, she has no place ruling a beauty pageant, let alone a whole plane of existence."

"Ah, so you do know her well." I smile affectionately, and Luc joins me.

"I will welcome your mother with open arms if she chooses to return, and I hope she will for your coronation."

"Before we get to that, the minute that Mabuz hears that an heir has been named, he will be here, throwing down a challenge." Ben's leg twitches with agitation, and Mason reaches across and cuffs his neck from behind, giving it a squeeze, which stops his leg immediately. I smother my lusty thoughts and focus on what he's saying.

"Fuck, I don't know if I can win against Imogen, but there is no way I can win against Mabuz. He has tricks up his sleeve I don't possess." I can't hide the worry in my voice, and Teddy grabs hold of my hand and squeezes it.

Luc, Levi, and Beezle exchange knowing glances. "While we were too late in locking down the portal, allowing our beautiful yet bothersome mate to escape, the minute I saw the mark, I made it so the portal couldn't be traveled through. There is no way he'll know about it before we are ready."

"Before you are ready?" Teddy questions, narrowing his gaze. "What exactly do you mean by that?"

Luc leans back and stretches like he doesn't have a care in the world, casually draping his arms along the back of the sofa. "Well, I couldn't hand over my crown to my beautiful and courageous niece with that kind of drama still hanging around. I am hoping that we can draw him to us on coronation day and dispatch his ass all before I put the crown on Glory's head, transferring my power to her—or that's what I want him to think."

"So she's bait?" Teddy growls, and I see Mason's hand tighten on Ben's neck. Ben winces slightly before Mason realizes and gentles his touch.

"Sort of, but I will make sure she is never at risk. I want the pleasure of dealing with my old friend myself."

"And what about all the people he has trapped or bargained with?" I ask, thinking about Bridgette, as well as Ben's friends and Mason's ex.

"Once I have the book back, I will be able to reverse all of his dirty spells. As for the humans, I will return them and wipe their minds. It will be as if it never happened."

"No!" I shout, standing up, and Luc frowns, losing his casual attitude.

"You don't want me to help them?" He sounds confused, and I don't blame him.

"There's only one I don't want you to help." I'm so agitated, I can't stay still. I move around the sitting room, looking at all the decorative trinkets, picking things up and putting them down again as I try to figure out how to explain what I want without appearing evil.

"What I think Glory is trying to find the right words to explain is that her daughters' mother is one of the humans who made a deal with Mabuz—Glory's life for her soul. If she can't have Nolan, then nobody can. I think Glory would prefer it if you didn't return Bridgette to her life, especially since they will all be living in Hell, and we don't want her asking any questions." Teddy is able to articulate exactly what I'm thinking.

"Yes, she is not getting her hands on my babies."

Lucifer's eyes widen comically. "You have babies? Where are they? Why have I not been allowed to smother them with Uncle Luc kisses?" He looks around the room like the girls are suddenly going to appear.

"They are Nolan's children from his relationship with Bridgette, but she is a horrible mother," I explain, smothering the smile that wants to appear.

Sometimes I can see the shrewd, intelligent man inside, and other times, he's the biggest himbo ever.

"I'd say. She put a hit on Glory and didn't care if they were caught in the cross fire," Mason grumbles, and Luc and his two lieutenants inhale gasps of shock and disgust.

"Fuck that. She will die at my hands," Leviathan declares, standing up and shocking the shit out of me.

"Why aren't they here? We will protect them with our lives," Beelzebub demands, also standing. "Do we need to send the legions to Earth to rescue them? Because we will."

"Holy shit," Ben mutters as all three men start planning a daring rescue that none of them can actually pull off. "They are losing it. Quick, Glory, do something."

"Whoa." I put my hands up, trying to settle the men, but it has no effect.

"Hey! Hey!" I shout and finally get their attention. "The girls are fine. They are with Nolan's parents here in Hell, which means they are safe for now, and as much as I like the idea of Bridgette dying, I'm not sure I can do that to the girls."

"Fine, she can rot in one of my cells until the girls are old enough to make the decision themselves," Luc concedes, and while I like that idea, that is still too close for comfort for me. What if she was able to escape?

"Can you completely mind wipe her, implant completely new memories so she doesn't remember the girls or Nolan, and send her back to Earth where she will never bother us again?" Teddy suggests, obviously uncomfortable with that plan as well.

"Yes, I can, and would everyone be okay with it if it happens to be a fairly miserable new memory?" Luc sounds a little sarcastic, but it will be good for him to learn to compromise now that he isn't going to be supreme ruler.

"Sounds perfect," I agree, and Leviathan and Beelzebub mutter obscenities under their breaths. I'm pretty sure that needs to happen sooner rather than later, because if we wait too long to deal with her, then they will take matters into their own hands, and my feelings won't be taken into consideration. Who would have thought that these two gruff giants would be gaga for children? Now I can only hope they catch up with Kerry and get her knocked up swiftly, because that would be entertainment worthy of popcorn.

"Okay, so I guess we have a plan for Mabuz, but we can go over it once I take care of Imogen. Now what about this coronation crap? What do I have to learn between now and then?

Luc smiles, and he looks at my men. "Can you guys give Glory and I a moment alone? Levi and

Beezle will take you to the palace pub for a few beers. We will catch up with you after."

All five of them leave. My three mates give me a kiss on the cheek on the way out, and to my amusement, Beezle and Levi do the same thing to Lucifer. It's so freaking cute, but I refrain from saying anything. I'm just glad that the three of them feel comfortable showing their relationship in front of us, because I don't think they do it often.

The door closes quietly behind them, and Luc waves a hand. I feel the magic activate, but I can't see any difference. He tugs on an ear. "You never know who is listening, and now, no one is."

"Whoa, will I be able to do that?" I ask him, and he nods.

"That and so much more, Glory. You will have more power than you can poke a stick at," he says smugly and situates himself back on the sofa, waving a hand and making two cocktails appear on the table in front of us. "Right, are you ready for the scoop?"

I pick up my drink and take a sip. It's a little bit tart and a little bit sweet and has a hell of kick—just like me, I would say.

"Hit me with it," I tell my uncle, bracing myself for what's to come.

Chapter Five

"I told you the creator is the one responsible for Heaven and Earth, but what I didn't tell you is who is responsible for Hell."

"By creator, do you mean God?" I ask, trying to make sense of everything, and he drops his chin.

"God's one name he's known by. Let's go with that to keep it simple. Firstly, they created Earth, allowing evolution to happen and bring about the existence of humans, but God always considered humans very flawed. He tried to instill good morals in them, but each new generation interpreted his word differently and made it fit their own agenda. He would rage and despair, even sent a flood to wipe them off the Earth at one stage, but my mother would have to remind him that he gave them free will and must allow them to make their own choices." Luc chuckles. "My father hated to be reminded, and it caused quite a bit of tension between him and my mother, so they decided to try again. They selected a few humans, humans with the right morality, as my father saw it, and they infused them with magic and created angels. They also had me and my siblings during this time, willing us to be angels as well." He stops to take a sip of his own cocktail, and I swallow roughly. I am certainly having my mind broadened today.

He sits back, a wrinkle on his brow as he thinks. "My personal opinion is that some of the humans they selected to be angels weren't as pious as he thought. I think my mother might have facilitated a few troublemakers just to keep the balance, hence the development of sins instead of virtue. They had an argument, and that's when I stepped in and offered to take the sinners and leave. Both Petra and I are like our mother, whereas Gabriel is the spitting image of Dad."

I'm so invested in the story, my cocktail is all but forgotten, but my stomach suddenly growls loudly, and Luc chuckles before waving a hand. A whole heap of snacks appears in front of me—pigs in blankets, chicken wings, little quiches, spring rolls, popcorn style chicken bites, and a bowl of fries. Next to them are a variety of dipping sauces. "Fuel yourself. We can't afford for you to be at anything less than your best."

"So what happened next?" I ask, taking his advice and placing a few things on a little plate that appeared next to everything.

"Well, Mom tried to argue that everything needed balance and that Dad was being unreasonable. He tried to smite her, and that's when she lost her shit. Different planes exist, sitting empty and waiting to be claimed, but they need a power source to become sustainable. Alone, she was not powerful enough to do this, she needed my father's help for that, so instead, she sacrificed herself, using all her power to give the sinners somewhere safe to live, away from the judgment and persecution of angels."

"Doesn't sound very angelic." I point a chip at him, and he snorts.

"Right?"

"So the Hell entity is..." I trail off because I think I know what he's going to say, but I want him to confirm it for me.

"My mother, Lilith," he confirms, smiling sadly, "and the powers I have access to are her powers. She can still use them, but she had to give up her corporeal form to make this happen." He waves an arm around, gesturing to Hell as a whole.

"Whoa!" I'm silent for a while as I process everything he just shared with me. That is some heavy shit.

"Would you like to meet her?" he asks, and I stop chewing and frown in confusion.

"What do you mean?" I ask around a mouthful before swallowing quickly.

"Come." He stands and holds out a hand. My gaze flicks to my food, and I mourn its loss. I really am hungry, and I hadn't even gotten to the wings yet.

"It will be there when we return, and it will be hot, I promise," Luc assures me, so I reach out and take his hand. I feel magic wash over me, and we appear in a large, rocky cavern. The heat is stifling, I wave a hand to try and cool myself, but it doesn't work.

"Why is it so hot in here?" I grumble, and he grins.

"Because we're sitting under Mt. Doom," Luc tells me, and I just gape at him.

"What the fuck?"

"To jump start this plane, I had to throw my corporeal body into the volcano, allowing my magic to flow out and over the land. Welcome, Glory, it is lovely to finally meet you." I turn around to find myself looking at the ghostly specter of the spitting image of my mother. Long, straight black hair flows down her back, and she has the same piercing green eyes as her children, but my mother has a softer look to her, like all her angles have been rounded. Lilith is slender, with only slight roundness to her breasts and hips.

"Holy shit," I mutter and rub my eyes, but nope, when I open them, she's still there. "You're the voice inside my head?"

"Yes, and trust me, she gets annoying," Luc says wryly, and I watch as Lilith, my grandmother, flips him off.

"You were never my favorite child," she says and pokes her tongue out, but he just grins.

"Liar."

"Have you told her what will happen when the power is handed over to her?" she asks, and Luc shakes his head.

"No, I thought it might be better coming from you."

"Okay, before I hand over the power of Hell to you, I would recommend sealing the bond with the gatekeeper. You may have noticed that Luc is a little, how shall I put this, erratic?" Lilith says, her spectral form floating around the room like she has too much energy—much like her son, I would guess.

It's Luc's turn to flip her off. "I'm not erratic, I'm bored, and I want to chase down my final mate. I was trying to push you into selecting an heir."

"And I was waiting for Glory. It was always going to be Glory. It was foretold."

"Why me?" I ask her, and she shrugs.

"Why not? Serena is lovely and all, but she's a little too much like your mother, and I've already had a lust demon in charge since the beginning, so it's time to change things up a little. Maybe you won't spend so much time fucking that you'll lose track of what you need to do. Maybe I can take a vacation from nagging and find a way to put myself back together, literally."

Damn! Lilith sounds as fed up as Luc is. She sighs.

"The power of Hell is a lot to deal with. Luc, being without mates for so many years, and not being bound to all of them, still didn't have enough power to be able to take all of mine, which means I had to stick around to take some of the burden off him, otherwise he would have gone nuts..." She pauses. "Even nuttier than he is."

I smother a chuckle and ignore the aghast look my uncle is giving his mother, though I have to say, I'm loving my family and forgive my mother for all of her crazy quirks now. She's practically normal compared to these two.

"But I fully expect you to be able to handle and control all of it, especially with it split across your seven mates."

Okay, now I'm paying attention. "That." I point at my grandmother. "What do you mean by that?"

"For example..." She rolls her eyes. "Luc declared the new mode of transportation in Hell to be Hell kangaroos, but he doesn't have enough juice to create them himself, and he relies on me to do it."

"Nope, like Mom said, I would be a puddle of

goo. That kind of power would fry my body. I'm not even sure if it were spread across the four of us if it would have been enough." He looks at his mom who shakes her head.

"No, which is why I made sure that Glory would have seven mates. The power will spread evenly across them, and none of them will suffer from the burden or go crazy. They will all have equal powers of creation."

"Julian is crazy enough as it is. He doesn't need to be crazier," Luc jokes, but I ignore him again.

"Are you responsible for Julian's meld with Cerberus?" I ask, and she nods.

"Yes, Cerberus was originally a way for Luc to share the burden when he hadn't found his mates. I didn't know how long it would take for them to come into existence, and I knew he wasn't going to be able to cope with the power solely, so when I threw myself into the volcano, Cerberus was my first creation. I didn't take into account that the power would wear away at him as well."

"Actually, he had some help. That blasted spell book and Mabuz expedited Cerberus's corporeal form's demise." Luc clenches his fists, and his eyes flash with ire.

Lilith's eyes widen. "I told you never to trust him. We need to get that book back from him. There is a spell in it that could unravel everything here on Hell. It's hidden, and it takes the blood from our bloodline to activate it, but all he has to do is get his hands on Petra or one of your siblings and it's over." Lilith sounds panicked.

"Holy crap, why haven't you ever said anything?" Luc accuses his mother, and she shrugs.

"I didn't think the little weasel had enough juice to power any of the spells, but if he's using human souls and blood to power them, then that would do it."

"We don't need blood to power the spells?" I ask, and she shakes her head while Luc just looks bemused.

"We don't?" he asks, and she chuckles this musical little tinkle that seems to float on the air.

"No, sweetheart. I told you that in the hopes it would discourage you from trying. I know how squeamish you are about blood."

"So you were setting him up and giving him a hand at the same time?" I ask, and she nods.

"Yes, I don't like to see my children fail, and although I was mostly certain he wouldn't use the really awful spells in that book, I wanted to ensure it."

"So how do we stop Mabuz?" I ask, and she and Luc exchange a glance, expressions of determination settling over both their faces.

"We kill him," she says plainly.

My stomach lurches despite me knowing they were going to say that.

"It's the only way to undo all the magic he's done. We want to release Mason's ex's soul from that Fabergé egg, not to mention any other souls he may have trapped. It will also undo the contracts the humans signed to give up their souls," Lucifer explains.

"You didn't tell Mason that earlier when you examined the egg."

"I didn't want your mate to go off in a rage."

"Good point," I concede, grateful for clear thinkers.

"It's one thing you're going to have to learn, Glory. As much as your emotions and empathy are going to make you a good queen, they are also going to be a hindrance. Sometimes you have to make decisions purely from a logical and practical point of view, and emotions can't cloud those judgments. It can get messy if they do. Also, while your mates will share the burden of power, you are the final decision-maker on everything. You can allow them to counsel you, but never let it be seen. You are the ultimate power. Executing Mabuz will show demons what will happen if anyone else gets delusions of grandeur."

A little squeak escapes my mouth. "You want me to kill him?"

They both nod. "Yes, if he comes for you, he will challenge you, which we are going to allow."

"What do you mean?" I ask, and Luc shrugs.

"I'm going to open the gates a few hours before the coronation and allow one of his minions to slip through and tell him. I expect he will make a big scene, bursting in to stop it, and challenge you at the last minute, but what he won't know is that you will have already been crowned queen."

I blink a couple of times. "I'm sorry, I think my lack of food has made me a bit dopey. Did you say I'd already be crowned queen?"

"Yes. The minute you seal that last bond with Julian, Luc will teleport you here, and we will do it in secret. The coronation will only be a show for everyone to see. That way, you can get a handle on your powers in private. It may be a little screwy to start with," Lilith cautions.

The little lurch in my stomach is a full-blown tsunami now, and I feel weak, like I'm going to throw up. I move over to one of the cave walls and lean my back against it, sliding down until I'm on the floor, pulling my knees up against my chest and hugging them.

"I think we broke her," my uncle tells his mother, and then I hear her shush him in return.

"Oh, honey, I know it's a lot to take in." I feel a ghostly hand brush across the top of my head. "Everything is going to be just fine, I promise."

"But how do I kill him?" I ask, and she smiles.

"With a thought. That's all you'll need. You will be that powerful."

"And don't think about going easy on Imogen either," Luc cautions me, and I look up at him, frowning.

"You're not worried that I'm going to kill your niece?" I ask, and he scoffs.

"Please. She would be an ideal candidate to jump into Mabuz's shoes, and what's worse, she's from the original bloodline. If she found the unravel spell, she could easily undo Hell and return to Heaven. She hates that she was cast out, and I'm almost certain she would be worse than Mabuz. She would subjugate all the demons and force them to deny their sins. In fact, it wouldn't surprise me if she is a plant sent by my father and brother."

Lilith huffs. "Yes, they are jealous of how well Hell runs, and the fact that we accept everyone as they are drives them crazy." She grins with undisguised glee. "I love that."

My head pounds with all the information I just learned and my future tasks. "I'm tired. Can we go back and eat? I also need a solid few hours of sleep before we do anything," I ask, and they exchange a worried glance.

"Of course. You take care of yourself, fuel up, and we will come up with a game plan to defeat Imogen." Luc holds out a hand to help me up, but I wave a hand at my uncle and climb to my feet unassisted.

"It's okay, I'm pretty certain I know how to handle her."

"Well, you just make sure the minute you do, you seal the bond with Julian so no one else can issue a mate challenge. They can still issue them, but they won't be able to kill you," he explains.

"And by then, we will have crowned you anyway, so there's no chance anyone will defeat you."

"And finally, I will be able to chase down my wayward mate." Luc grins, and I think about Kerry. Poor girl doesn't have a chance. She doesn't even know he can leave Hell. I'll have to get word to her somehow.

"Can my mom be at the coronation?" I ask, desperate to have my family there. If I can't leave, I want them to come and go as they please.

"Of course. I'll go to Earth and escort her back myself if I have to," my uncle assures me.

"Okay, well, I guess we'll see you soon," I say to my grandmother, feeling awful that she's trapped here.

She must hear what I'm thinking. "Don't worry, Glory. Once I hand over the power to Hell, I will no longer be trapped."

"And what will happen to you?"

She shrugs. "I don't really know, but I'm hoping

returning to the universe will allow me to repower and reform a corporeal body, but I guess time will tell."

"What are you?" I ask as Luc takes my hand, and she smiles serenely.

"I am life, Glory," she whispers as we teleport back to the palace.

Chapter Six

When Luc and I return to his palace, we arrive in a garden with a pretty little marble fountain. The fountain is a sculpture of Lilith, and she is on her knees, weeping. It's sad and poignant, and I'm dying to ask him why she was crying, but I have a feeling it's not a subject for now. The garden is like a little paved Italian piazza, with bushes with stunning flowers I don't recognize, but they are in a rainbow of colors, similar to a tulip when it has opened up.

"You can share everything you learned with your mates. I don't want you to keep secrets from them, but you must not share what you know with anyone else, including your mother. As far as she is aware, our mother sacrificed herself when she kick-started this plane. Petra can't know that she is still here in spirit."

"Why not? That's her mother. I would want to know that my mother was around."

Luc nods sadly. "Yes, but because she isn't the

heir or the heir mates, she wouldn't be able to see or hear her anyway, and that would just be devastating. Maybe once Mom has turned the power over to you and goes wherever it is she will go, and maybe if she can rejuvenate a corporeal form, then she will return, but until then, as far as Petra knows, our mother gave her life for us and demon kind."

I screw up my nose in annoyance but agree. "I hate lying to my mother, but I understand. She won't hear about it from me or any of my mates."

"Good. I will send someone to retrieve her, your fathers, and siblings and bring them here before your coronation."

"Not before the mate challenge?" I cock my head to the side. "Are you worried I'm going to lose?"

"Pfft, no," he disagrees vehemently, but I can see a shadow of worry. "But I don't want you distracted by any of them."

"Okay, you make a good point. Fine. I'm going to head back to my room to rest and recharge and come up with a plan for tomorrow's challenge."

"Are you okay if I announce that it will be held at the colosseum?" he asks me.

"In Rome?" I exclaim, and he chuckles, shaking his head.

"No, we have a replica here in Dante's Inferno."

My mouth drops open, and I gape at him.

"This city is called Dante's Inferno? Are you freaking serious?"

He shrugs. "Just because we're on a different plane, it doesn't mean I don't keep up with everything earthbound. And yes, this decade it is. Last decade it was called Middle Earth. You'll have to start a list. That's what I do every time I come up with a new and interesting name for something."

"No, just no. I don't even have time for you and your nonsense at the moment. I am going to get my eat on and then hopefully my freak on, and then I will get my fight on. I will see you in the morning."

"TMI, Glory, TMI," my uncle calls out from behind me, but I don't even bother looking back. I'm done, and I just want to find my mates. My head is reeling, and I have to tell them everything I learned. I can only hope and pray that they have sorted their shit out, and I don't have to listen to them bicker anymore.

I have no idea where my mates are. I'm assuming that they are in the room we chose, and if they've all gone their separate ways, then I will take advantage of some quiet time and see if this place has a bathtub.

To my surprise, the room is empty, but I find a quickly scrawled note on the little coffee table.

Glory, we have gone to the club called Seven Circles. It's not far from the palace. We can find what we all need to

satisfy our sins there. You're welcome to join us if you want
—Carter

P.S. Nolan and Julian sorted out their shit. You won't
have any problems from either of them.

I breathe out a sigh of relief at that last sentence. I was worried the two of them were going to hold onto their animosity, and it was going to cause a real problem. That's one less thing I need to worry about.

Do I want to join them though? I'm hungry and tired and a little out of sorts, not to mention reeling from meeting my grandmother—or her spirit anyway—and learning that it's her who powers Hell and turned Luc a little bit crazy. How can she be sure that I won't be the same? How can she be sure that the power will spread evenly across me and my mates? It's a lot to put my faith in. And what was that last comment? She is life? What does that make her, a god? I guess that would make sense. Apparently, I'll be able to do anything with just a thought, including kill someone. That's going to take some getting used to. No more imagining random shit, otherwise, it may literally come to fruition.

I look around the room, feeling a little lost. It's the first time I've been alone in ages. I can't decide if I want to cry or do a happy dance. My eyes flit longingly to the bed. I could just climb in and close my eyes and sleep the whole night through, but then my stomach rumbles and I groan. Damn it, Luc promised me I could finish off the snacks, and I forgot and flounced off instead.

I guess that answers my question then. I'm going to have to go out and find the guys. If they have everything sins need at the club, then I will be able to find food.

I look down at my jeans and shirt and decide that even though I don't know what kind of club it is, I'm going to have to put in a little more effort.

I spend the next half hour changing and putting on my makeup. The teal green body-con dress I'm wearing doesn't hide a single one of my curves, and I love it. It stops at mid-thigh and has a plunging neckline. I know some people would say it's not appropriate for a woman with my curves, but I don't care. I work hard to maintain my figure, and I love it even if it is thicker than some. A pair of Spanx helps keep my stomach flat in the dress, but apart from that, the rest is all me.

I'm about to step out the door when I stop suddenly. Shit, the mate challenge. What if she's lying in wait for me somewhere to knock me off when I don't expect it? Maybe I should stay home. I'm torn between going and staying. Luc said we were safe in this wing of the house but didn't mention anything else. I don't want to be the idiot who takes a risk and blows everything. I peer out the door and startle. The two guards who previously flanked Luc's room are flanking mine.

"Ms. Luxure." One of them bows his head. "His Royal Highness said we were to accompany you if you wished to go anywhere. He said you may decide to join your mates at Seven Circles. We are to go along until you are in their company to ensure you get there safely."

"Thank you, Uncle Luc," I mutter under my breath, my dilemma solved for me. Smiling, I step out of the room.

"Excellent. Would you please lead the way?" I request, and it takes them a small moment to react. Both of them are unable to hide their interest quickly. It makes a girl feel good when men who are not her mates look at her like that, but they are professionals, so they swiftly return their expressions to resting bitch face.

"Follow us please." The other guard takes the lead with the first one taking up a place at my back. Do I feel a trickle of unease? Yes, but I have to hope and pray both of these guys are loyal to Luc. I don't think they would be guarding his room if they weren't. I don't have a weapon, and I'm certainly not quick enough to use the spell to call the interdimensional cubby and grab one from Ben's space. Actually, come to think of it, I didn't see any, but I guess one of those wig heads could be used in a pinch. I need the guys, especially Mason, to key me into theirs. I'm pretty sure he and Teddy would have exactly what I need. Even Carter and Nolan may, but I think they probably got used to carrying their weapons for human sensibilities on Earth, since it wouldn't do for them to pull something out of supposed thin air.

We take the same limo that brought us to the palace to the club. It's a short drive, but there is a huge line out front when we arrive, and I groan. I shouldn't have worried, though, because when the doormen see the royal guards exit the car, they are more than happy to allow me to skip the line. I hear whispers behind me.

"Who's that?"

"Is that the king's limo?"

"Do you think the king has found his mate?"

"Nah, I bet it's just the flavor of the month."

"I heard that he and his two lieutenants are very close, if you know what I'm saying."

The whispers fade away as I enter the foyer of the club. In front of me is a bank of elevators. I frown and look around. This building was only two stories, so why would they need a bank of elevators? A hostess approaches me with a welcoming smile on her face, and the two guards step a little closer to me.

"Welcome to the Seven Circles of Hell. Which sin will be your pleasure tonight?" She spouts off what sounds like a script, but I get that.

"Weren't there nine circles of Hell?" I ask, and

her smile drops, and she bites her lip, looking at the two guards on either side of me.

"We don't talk about that," she says nervously, and one of the guards snorts.

"The rumors go that Lucifer didn't like Dante's version of Hell. He said it was ridiculous when we all know there are only seven sins. He only used four of them and made up the rest of his crap. I think if he could have left Hell, he probably would have marched up to Dante and punched him in his face."

"Hence Seven Circles of Hell. So what will be your pleasure tonight?" She resumes her composure when the guards do nothing to punish me or her. Okay, good to know. If I ever want to get a rise out of my uncle, I can bring up Dante's circles of Hell.

I can tell they are waiting for me to decide, but I'm torn. Do I take care of my own sin first before I start searching for the others? Carter better not be taking care of his unless it's with one of my other mates. Lust or gluttony? The others are fine without me for a little while.

"Gluttony please." I trust Carter, so I need to take care of my own needs first.

She beams. "Fabulous. So you are on the limbo level. You need to go down to level two for gluttony." She waves her hands at the bank of elevators like a game show host. "Enjoy your visit, and be sure to have fun."

She turns and heads back to her little alcove.

"Well, okay then. Are you accompanying me?" I ask the two guards who shake their heads.

"No, we were told to make sure you got safely into the elevator. Luc just alerted us that Imogen is still in the palace, so you should be fine."

I frown, confused, I didn't see any of them answer a phone.

One of them taps the side of their head. "Telepathy," he explains.

"Oh, well, that makes things easy."

"You would think so, but he gets bored and likes to fuck with us. He'll hum a catchy tune in our heads and then exit, leaving us with a damn ear worm for most of the day."

I chuckle, shaking my head at another story about my deranged uncle. "Well, I promise not to do that," I assure them. "At least not for the first ten years."

I giggle as they exchange a glance, and I step into the elevator and press the button for the second level. I give them a finger wave as the doors close, amused at their wry expressions. I mean, I wouldn't want them to get bored and complacent. I have to keep them on their toes somehow.

I had no idea what to expect of the different levels. I thought about asking the two guards but decided I wanted to come in with an open mind. To say that I'm surprised when the doors open is an understatement. I'm not sure exactly what I was expecting, but this was not it. I step out, and another hostess approaches me as I look around the room in amazement. It is set up to look like a high-class restaurant, but instead of tables and chairs, there are little sunken booth-like enclosures. I guess, depending on what you choose, they are set up to either have tables and chairs or an empty space. What is the empty space for? I look around, but none of the empty spaces are currently being used. Some of the tables are occupied by guests who all seem to be enjoying mountains of food.

"Hello, what is your pleasure this evening? Would you like to partake in the buffet?" She waves her hand to the side of the room where a lavish buffet spread has been laid out for people to help themselves. "Or would you like to select from our special menu?" She produces a leather bound menu from behind her back and holds it out to me.

"What's on the special menu?" I ask her, and she smiles this secret little smile.

"Never been here before?" she asks, and I shake my head.

"No, actually, I haven't." She claps her hands, smacking the menu between them, and she bounces on the spot.

"Oh, I do like a virgin. The special menu allows you to choose whatever you would like to splosh in."

"Sploshing?" I think I know what she means,

but it could mean something different in Hell than on Earth.

"Covering yourself in whatever food you want," she replies, and I frown.

"Isn't it a sexual thing? I don't have a partner."

She shrugs. "We get solo people all the time. Gluttony demons don't seem to need a partner to become aroused by food."

I arch an eyebrow. "No, I guess you're not wrong." I look around the room and bite my lip, not sure about what to choose. The sploshing sounds fun, but not on my own.

"Can I take a name for the booking?" the girl asks while she waits for me to make a decision.

"Gloriana Luxure," I tell her, and her eyes widen slightly.

"Oh, I'm sorry, Ms. Luxure, your party has been waiting for you in a private room. If you'll just follow me this way."

She places the menu back on the podium next to the door and hurries off across the restaurant. I feel a thrill of excitement as I follow after her. Hopefully she is leading me to one of my guys. If it's not them, and someone is waiting to kill me, then they will feel the full wrath of my demon, because I am sick of having my meals interrupted.

Chapter Seven

S he leads me in the opposite direction of the buffet, past all the tables and sploshing pits, and toward a hallway. "This is where all our private dining rooms are for those who want to fuck, though people are welcome to fuck in the sploshing pits as well. We don't kink shame in Seven Circles."

I want to giggle at her words, but I don't. It's so refreshing to be able to let our freak flags fly without having to worry about condemnation. I could sit and eat as much as I want for as long as I want and never hear any shame like I did from those women at Tasty Treats. They were a couple of judgy bitches, considering they were demons as well.

Huh, I bet they are going to be surprised next time they return to Hell to find me in charge. Maybe I should send them a royal welcome. It's going to be fun to be queen once I wrap my head around the whole godlike powers thing. I also kind of get why Luc makes crazy decisions.

She stops outside one of the closed doors. "Just in here first." She opens a door, and it's a gorgeously appointed bathroom. "In the cubbies, you will find some paper underwear if that's what you wish. Just strip and put them on or go naked. Whatever you feel like really. Put your clothes and purse in a cubby. You can lock them and put the key wristband on your wrist. Grab one of the robes, and then I can show you to your meal."

I go in and quickly do as she says, my excitement building at not knowing what I'm going to find.

I decide to forgo the paper underwear, since it looks like there are showers available for when I'm done. Tying the key around my wrist, I toe off my heels and pad barefoot back to the hallway where the hostess is waiting for me.

"Here, I thought you may like this." She holds out a hair tie.

"Good thinking, thank you." I use it to tie my long hair back in a ponytail, and she leads me farther down the hall.

"Your party is waiting for you inside." She winks. "I'm a little jealous. They are certainly a feast for the senses." She turns and walks away, but not before I notice an envy designation on her hand. Well, she's going to have to find her own feast, because these ones are mine. I wonder who is in there, and if it's all of them or just a couple.

I push the door open and stop dead in my tracks. It's a sunken circular room with two steps down. The pit is covered in cakes and desserts. Trifles, jellies, cream-filled cakes, and more cover the whole surface of the pit in a vibrant display of color and flavor, and right in the center of it all are Louis and Carter. Both of them are naked and have whipped cream dotted over their torsos, and Carter's leads down to his cock. Louis's cock is actually clean, and Carter has a little whip cream smeared across his mouth.

I put my hands on my hips. "Did you two start this party without me?"

Carter shrugs. "Can you blame me? Look at him. His banana split was so tempting." I giggle and throw off my robe before descending the steps. I pause and look around, trying to find a path through the desserts, but I can't see one.

Louis suddenly jumps up and steps through it, not caring that he's destroying the beautifully displayed desserts. He grabs hold of me and drags me back to where Carter is waiting. "We're here to make a mess, so we might as well get started," he says, his accent thick with desire. I'm surprised to find that everything is on a mattress of some kind that has a bit of give. He passes me down to Carter before joining us, the movement making all the desserts wobble around us. Carter spreads me out on a mound of cakes, and I shudder as my body sinks into the cold yet strangely erotic desserts.

They squish between my toes and butt crack, and a small squeal escapes my lips at the feel of them smooshing around my body. I start to giggle uncontrollably. "Oh my god, that feels…" I trail off, and Carter grins.

"Gross but weirdly amazing, right?"

"So gross, but so good," I agree as he holds up a smushed bit of cake and feeds it to me.

"Holy crap." I moan as the flavor hits my taste buds. "They are fucking delicious."

"They really are," Louis agrees as he starts to spread cake and desserts all over my body, "and we can't wait to eat it directly from your body."

The two of them use me as a canvas, spreading food all over me before leaning down and using their mouths to clean me up. Louis is paying very close attention to my breasts. I watch as he grabs a handful of red jelly from a bowl and drips globs of it over my nipples, the cold making them pucker into tight little nubs.

"I do love raspberry," he says, leaning in and latching his lips around one of the tight peaks, sucking hard before using his tongue to clean up the rest of the jelly before moving to the other side. My giggles turn to moans, and I squirm on the spot, my body sliding back and forth through the mess.

Carter is a man on a mission, and he's spread

what looks like tiramisu all over my bare mound and is about to shove his finger in when I reach down and stop him. "Wait," I say, trying to sit up but only succeeding in raising my head.

"What's wrong?" He looks down at the mound of dessert in his hand before looking back at me.

"I don't want to get a UTI," I tell him, and his brows crease.

"A what?" he asks, and I feel myself blush.

"You know, a urinary tract infection. The sugar in that will definitely be bad."

His brows straighten, and both guys chuckle. "We're demons, remember? No pesky human infections for us."

"Huh, really?" I ask, and Louis shrugs.

"We're disgustingly healthy. Apart from Hell mumps, which I'm pretty sure your uncle created just for fun, and Hell flu, we don't get sick—unless, of course, we neglect our sin and try to use our powers. That's what Hell flu is."

I think back to my childhood, and he's right. I don't ever remember feeling sick unless I hadn't topped up on my sin. "Huh. Well, okay then, carry on."

He smears the dessert all over my pussy, even shoving his fingers deep inside me, and my eyes roll back in my head. The cold is such a contrast to how fucking hot the rest of me is, it's a fucking religious experience. "Oh my god," I whimper as he starts to eat it with his mouth.

"No, baby, you can just call me Carter." The idiot lifts his head and winks, so I grab it with both hands and shove it down.

"Less talking, more eating," I tell him. Louis chuckles and brings a spoon of something up to my mouth. I open it, and he zooms it in like an airplane. Great, two idiots.

Whatever he fed me is rich and chocolatey and decadent, and instead of scolding him, another feral sound leaves my mouth. Holy fuck, I never want to have sex any other way again. Goosebumps break out across my flesh, and a shiver runs all the way down my spine, making my pussy pulse with need.

Carter, who has cleaned off all the cake, lifts something up that makes my eyes widen.

"What are you going to do with that?" I ask him, although I'm pretty certain I know. It's one of those long, twisted lollipops.

"What do you think?" He wears a wicked grin, and he sticks it into his mouth, and my eyes widen with shock as he deep throats it.

"Holy fuck," I mutter as he drags it back out.

"You didn't think you were the only talented one in this family, did you?" he asks before notching it at the entrance of my pulsing, needy pussy.

"Louis, how about you do something about that

mouth?" Carter suggests and starts to slide it into my aching core.

"Fuck!" I throw my head back, the cake squishing through my hair as the twisted lollipop slides in and out of my pussy, rubbing my inner walls in all the right places. A tap on my mouth has me opening my eyes and groaning as Louis feeds me his trifle-covered cock. I go to town, placing one hand on his hip to hold him exactly where I want him. I slurp and suck, unconcerned by the enthusiastic sounds that come out of my mouth.

"Glory, my little cream cake, you are a wonder," Louis mutters, stroking his hand through my dessert streaked hair.

Once I've cleaned off his dick, I use his hip to drag him closer and feed his cock down my throat. There is no way I'm going to let Carter win this one. I am woman enough, though, to admit it is a struggle to concentrate and do a decent job of taking care of Louis while Carter shoves that lollipop in and out and laps my clit. My toes curl, and I stop paying attention to Louis. I arch my back as a searing bolt of pleasure bursts through me, and I scream.

"Carter, fuck."

He plunges that lollipop in and out in long strokes, flicking daintily at my clit with his tongue, while my core tries to hold onto it. Tears leak from my eyes, and I thrash my head back and forth.

"That's one. Let's prep you for us now, okay?" he says, moving the sucker from my pussy and pressing it against my puckered asshole. I feel my body tighten. "Oh no, don't you get all tense on me now. Louis, fuck her mouth and distract her while I prep her ass, then we can fuck both her holes while we roll around in this mess."

I shudder at Carter's words, his voice deep and husky as he uses his hand to lube the lollipop with some jelly before pressing it against my tight hole. I lose sight of him as Louis straddles my torso and dumps a large portion of cream-filled sponge on my chest before smoothing it all over my breasts. "Fuck, I've dreamed of doing this to you, Glory." His pupils are pinpricks of desire. I guess he's as turned on as I am, being a fellow gluttony demon. He licks his lips and grins as he pushes my breasts together and slowly slides his cock through the creamy cake mess.

"Mon Dieu," he mutters as my tongue flicks across the tip of his cock as he thrusts forward, licking what I can off before he slides back. He shuffles forward a little more and pushes my breasts even farther up, and this time when he thrusts, I open my mouth, and he slides in. I create suction before he slides back out again.

Carter gently slides the lollipop into my ass, and my mouth falls open. I'm useless against the onslaught of sensations. Louis uses my mouth and thrusts in time with Carter. I writhe under the onslaught of pleasure, trapped between these two men, a prisoner to their exquisite torture.

My breathing gets faster, my heartbeat rises like it's going to explode out of my chest, and the words coming out of my mouth are nonsensical. I'm so close to falling off that perfect precipice again when Carter stops what he's doing and pulls the lollipop out, throwing it off to the side and stopping Louis mid-thrust. "She's ready for us," he tells my French mate. Louis rolls off me, pulling me on top of him. I slip and slide, but he finally has me where he wants me. As he presses his lips to mine, tangling our tongues in a kiss full of fire, he thrusts his dick deep into my cunt.

"Ugh." I can't do anything but groan at the feeling. A hand on my back keeps me leaning forward, and Louis holds himself deep as Carter presses himself into my ass in a slow and steady push.

"Good girl," he croons as I breathe out, pressing back into him, desperate to feel them both inside me.

"Oh fuck." He presses balls deep, and I feel stuffed and fucking amazing. Knowing I'm giving pleasure to both of my mates is the ultimate high. I'm a little giddy and delirious now, and all I can do is hold on and enjoy the ride. Carter pulls out and then thrusts back in, while Louis alternates his rhythm. Their hard, thick lengths set a punishing pace, lighting every single nerve on fire. They push me higher, my lungs struggling to take in air as ecstasy flows through me. I'm unable and unwilling to escape the onslaught of passion. Building in the very center of my core, a white-hot shot of lightning flashes through my body in a spine tingling, toe curling bolt of pleasure, and I scream before burying my face in Louis's shoulder and clamping down hard with my teeth. I hear him grunt then groan as he stills, filling me with his cum. Carter lasts a couple more thrusts and moans loudly, praising us both and exalting his love as he, too, fills me with his cum.

Sweat mixes with exotic desserts as the three of us heave, our breathing ragged and our pulses racing. It probably takes us a good five minutes to calm down and get our breathing back to normal. Carter pulls out and disappears, leaving Louis and I to untangle ourselves. We giggle as our bodies stick together and make a squelching noise as we pull apart.

I flop back next to him, and we both stare up at the ceiling, our breathing still a little shaky.

"Wow," I rasp out, and he chuckles, reaching over to hold my hand.

"You can say that again, my little biscuit."

I look around our feast and find a spot where the desserts are undamaged. I see donuts, and my stomach rumbles. I roll over and crawl across to grab a couple before returning to Louis. I hold one out to him, and he takes it, groaning with as much pleasure as he had while we were fucking.

"The dessert chef here is superior. I must make an appointment to meet with him," he says after swallowing his mouthful.

"Meh, he's okay, but not as good as you," I reply after finishing off my treat.

Carter returns. "Come on, you two. Let's shower and then go find our other mates."

"What, you don't want to lie around and snuggle with us?" I pout playfully as he screws up his nose.

"Don't get me wrong, that was fun and I'd gladly come back with you any day, but no, cake between my ass cheeks is not a fun sensation."

My pout turns to a glare. "Yet you felt compelled to use it as lube," I point out, trying to sit up, but I keep slipping.

"Ah, but I beg to differ. I used the jelly," he argues, holding out a hand to first help me up and then Louis.

"Potayto, potahto," I reply as I throw my cake-covered body around his clean one. He must have showered off before coming to get us.

"Glory!" he yelps, and Louis joins in the fun, sandwiching him between us.

"Looks like you're going to have to shower again," I sing, and he mutters under his breath,

pushing us away and stomping back to the bathroom that is off to the side of the pit.

Louis and I follow gleefully along behind him.
This has been so much fun, I can't wait to do it
again. I wonder who I can con into coming back
with me. I bet Mason will be up for it, but I'm not
sure about the rest. I'll have to wait and see.

Chapter Eight

The three of us make use of the showers before we redress and go in search of the others. In between soaping each other up, they explained about each level. Apparently, the greed level is a high-end shopping mall, the wrath level is a fighting ring, the pride level contains an art gallery and showroom, the envy level is a dance and performance club full of beautiful, talented people, the lust level is a brothel and BDSM club, and finally, the sloth level has a whole heap of sleep pods and gaming suites.

First, we're heading to the wrath level. Nolan needed to get a handle on his sin. Although he and Julian talked everything out and have forgiven one another, he still needed to blow off steam. To my surprise, they didn't angry fuck. Louis said they weren't ready to establish that part of their relationship yet, and I'm certainly not going to force it. The seven of them have to get there organically without help from me.

That left Nolan needing an outlet. Apparently, Nolan is interested in the fighting ring and used to fight regularly in college. I'm actually excited to see it. It won't hurt for people to know I have a lethal mate once my heir status becomes common knowledge.

The doors open, and we are greeted by a screaming, cheering crowd. In the middle of the big arena is a large fight cage, and inside are two men who are wailing on each other.

"Holy fuck," I mutter, and Louis and Carter lead me through the tiered seats to a row right in front of the octagon-shaped cage. There, I find Mason and Teddy cheering.

"Ah, there you are, princess." Mason pats the empty chair next to him. "Come and watch Nolan. He really is magnificent." He has a few shopping bags at his feet, so I guess he got his sin on earlier. I give him a quick kiss before leaning over him and giving Teddy one too. Mason's hand slips up my dress and cups my ass cheek, giving it a quick squeeze. "Did you have fun?" he asks, and I nod, but I'm looking carefully at my pride demon to make sure he took care of his needs too.

"Are you okay?" I ask him, and he hauls me over Mason and situates me in his lap, nuzzling into my neck.

"Sure am. Mason's pride in Nolan's ability

could fill me up, but I also went to the pride level and displayed my bike collection."

"Your bike collection?" I ask, not sure what he is talking about.

"Yeah, I have a collection of vintage motorcycles that can't be found here in Hell. I had them stored in my interdimensional space, so I brought them out. The demons admired them a lot and filled me up within minutes. I'm good for at least a week, but I'll leave them there for now and go back every time I need to fuel up."

Huh, so that's how that works. That's smart. "Where are Ben and Julian?" I ask, making myself comfortable in Teddy's lap. His fingers play with the hem of my dress as his attention returns to the fight.

"Julian is taking a nap on the sloth level, and Ben headed off to the envy level. I'm not sure exactly what he's doing," Mason answers while Louis and Carter take the spare seats.

"How's he doing?" Carter asks Mason before I can say anything.

"He's toying with his opponent. It's been fun up until now, but the crowd is starting to get rowdy."

Louis rolls his eyes. "Trust Nolan to make the crowd angry as well. He won't need to feed for weeks either."

My eyes dart to the men in the ring. I hadn't been paying close enough attention, but sure enough, my wrath demon is in there. He's wearing the tiniest pair of shorts and glistens with sweat. His eyes glow red with wrath, and he has a slightly split lip.

"Looks like his opponent got a shot in." I nod at his lip, and Mason scoffs.

"Nolan let him have false hope. Trust me, that guy was never going to win, and I am going to make a pretty penny off our mate when he finally stops being a bitch and finishes it!" He shouts the last bit, and Nolan's head whips around to face us. I wave at him, and a cocky grin crosses his lips as he pushes his hair back from his face, and I feel my gluttonous pussy pulse with joy. It doesn't matter that I just got fucked five ways to Sunday by Carter and Louis, she wants a piece of Nolan now too.

He winks at me, and I blow him a kiss just as his opponent tackles him to the ground. I wince. "Is that allowed?" I ask, and I feel Teddy nod behind me.

"Yeah, apparently demon ring fights have no rules, except no use of powers other than speed and strength, which they both have. It's kind of brutal."

I watch on in horror as Nolan's opponent punches him twice in the head. Gasping, I slap a hand over my mouth to stop from crying out.

"Hey, it's fine, I promise. Watch." Mason pats me on the knee, not taking his eyes off the fight as Teddy's hand creeps a little higher up my dress to brush against the seam of my panties. "Good thinking, Teddy. Keep our girl distracted while our boy makes me some money."

Mason leans forward and pulls a plush, super soft blanket out of the bag and tosses it over us. "I bought that for Julian, to welcome him to the group," he tells me, nodding at it, "but I'm sure he won't mind if you use it for a little while." Aww, how fucking sweet is Mason? He's such a softy.

Teddy doesn't wait any longer now that we've been covered by the blanket. He uses a finger to push my panties to the side, swiping a finger through my pussy.

"You're just like a filled donut with a sticky sweet center. Did our boys take good care of you?" he whispers in my ear, and my nipples pebble under my dress. Even though I showered, I'm not surprised I have the combined fluids of Carter and Louis leaking out of me. They certainly filled me with enough.

He plays with the mess leaking out of me, thrusting it in and out a bit, before dragging his fingers up and circling my clit. "Watch your mate make mincemeat out of that loser. I want to hear you cheering and shouting for Nolan while I make you come."

I bite my lip to stop myself from crying out, but Teddy slaps my clit, and I gasp. "I want to hear you cheer for your mate."

I can't believe he's being bossy. Isn't he supposed to be the submissive one?

Mason chuckles. "I think you shocked our mate, Teddy. She was expecting soft, pliant, and submissive, but you're all riled up from the fight. I think he'd like to hop in the ring for a few rounds himself and work off some aggression." Mason doesn't take his eyes off the fight for a moment. "You better do what he says, and next time I have him tied up, you can have your revenge."

Teddy stops what he's doing, so I cup my hands around my mouth and shout, "Go, Nolan, woo-hoo!" The man in question bucks his opponent off and throws him across the arena where he stumbles and goes down hard.

As Nolan waits for him to recover, he stalks over to us, putting his hands on the wire, and peers down at us. He arches an eyebrow at seeing the blanket over my lap before a wicked grin crosses his mouth, and he points at Teddy. "You make sure she's screaming for me, okay?" He winks and turns back to his opponent.

"With pleasure," Teddy rumbles behind me and places a kiss against my neck before nipping it, causing goosebumps to rise on my skin. His hand drifts away from my clit, and I feel him reach under me to fiddle with the zipper of his jeans before lifting his hips and shimmying down a little. Holy shit, is he going to fuck me here in the front row of the arena with thousands of people around us? He maneuvers me, and sure enough, lifts me and slides me down his thick length. He thrusts up until I'm seated completely on his cock.

"Oh my god," I shout, not worried about who hears me because Nolan just got hit again. They are going to think I'm shouting about him. Teddy nibbles my ear before nipping the lobe. "Lean forward, babe, and ride my cock while you cheer on your mate." He pushes my back slightly, and I put my feet on the ground, leaning forward like I'm enthralled with the match, then I start to bounce up and down, cheering and shouting.

"Yes, that's it! Fuck him up," I scream at my mate who is wailing on his opponent. I'm so fucking turned on by everything that I feel my orgasm start tingling in my toes as the pleasure starts to seep out through my body, slowly rising upwards. I press my hands against Teddy's solid knees to get better leverage and swirl my hips around, and I smile as I hear Teddy grunt behind me. My pussy pulses, and I cheer harder for Nolan.

"Fuck yes, do it just like that, harder, damn it!" I yell, and Teddy listens, his thrust getting more exaggerated as his hand slips down to play with my clit.

The sounds of flesh on flesh drive me frantic. "Yes, that's it, so fucking close," I call out, and I see Nolan grin wickedly as he hauls his fist back and drives one last face breaking punch into his opponent as Teddy pinches my clit, driving me over the edge. I free fall and scream as my nerve endings light on fire and my body soars.

"Yes, yes, yes," I chant as everyone around me screams and shouts as Nolan's opponent is left bloody and unconscious in the middle of the octagon.

Teddy grunts and joins me as I lean back and wrap my arm around his neck, turning my head to pull him in to kiss me. I feel his cock pulse as he fills me with his cum.

The crowd is on their feet, cheering for the victor, as the ref declares Nolan the winner and a team of what must be medical personnel run out to check on the loser who's lying lifeless on the floor of the cage.

"Is he dead?" I ask, my breathing still out of control from Teddy's handiwork.

We watch on in silence as they check for a pulse, and a sense of relief shudders through me as they give the thumbs-up. I didn't want to see him die, he did try his hardest, but Nolan was a fucking animal. I know I just came, but now I want to ride Nolan like he's a fucking pony.

He stalks over to the edge of the cage and looks down at me. His lip and eyebrow are bleeding, and his eyes still glow with wrath. He looks like he'd throw me down in the middle of the cage and fuck me in front of all of these demons if he could reach me. I can't say I hate the idea, but maybe it's best that they don't know how their future queen moans in the middle of an orgasm despite having done exactly that, but it was disguised.

"Changing rooms, now!" he shouts down at me and points across the room.

"Okay, let's get you moving." Mason stands up and offers me a hand. Teddy quickly lifts me up and lets my panties fall back into place as he tucks himself back into his pants before pulling my dress down to make me presentable. He whips off the blanket as I stand up and folds it up like nothing X-rated just happened underneath it, and calmly stuffs it back into the bag Mason pulled it from. He leans in and gives me a kiss.

"Have fun." He winks. Mason takes my hand and leads me out of our aisle. Carter and Louis both give me kisses on the way past.

"He may be a while, since his fans will want to congratulate him, but we don't want to keep him waiting. His wrath demon still seems to be riding him hard. I swear wrath, lust, and gluttony demons have it so much harder than the rest of us," he says close to my ear so I can hear him above the crowd still chanting and cheering. No one pays any attention as the two of us walk down the space between the seats toward a door in the back of the arena that says, "Staff only." Mason pushes through, and we enter another wide corridor with doors on either side.

"The changing rooms are over here." We walk the distance in silence, comfortable enough with each other for it not to be awkward. He stops and opens a door that says, "Men," on it. I brush past him on the way in and feel his erection brush against me. I look down and arch an eyebrow in surprise.

"What? You looked hot coming all over Teddy's lap, plus I just made a fortune because of Nolan. It's been a great night."

"Well, how about we make it an amazing night, and I take care of that while we wait?" I grab his hand and drag him into the changing rooms with me. I'm riding the high of an orgasm and watching the sheer brutality of my mate overcome his opponent, and I'm still horny as fuck.

Pushing him up against one of the walls, I unzip his jeans, pull his erection out of his hands, and run my tongue up and down it like a lollipop.

"Fuck, Glory!" His knees buckle slightly before he braces them, and his hands tangle in my hair. I smile, liking this change of dynamic. Don't get me wrong, I am super happy to play whatever domination games he wants, but sometimes a girl likes to feel powerful too.

My panties are a mess as my core contracts with want. I get down on my knees and wrap my lips around the head of his cock, hollowing my cheeks and sucking. I do this a couple of times, going lower each time while using my tongue to massage underneath his length. His hands tighten in my hair, and he starts to thrust gently back and forth.

"Your mouth feels so good. Hot and wet and mine. That's a good girl, take it a little deeper," he coaxes.

Bit by bit, I get closer and closer to his pelvis, his cock sliding down my throat with every pass until I finally have it all. I breathe through my nose as it presses against his pelvis, tears running down my face as he holds me in place.

"Swallow, baby," he encourages me, and I do, my throat constricting around his dick, and he grunts.

"Fuck yeah, that feels amazing."

The door to the changing rooms suddenly slams open. I try to pull away, but he tightens his grip and holds me in place. I start to struggle a little, and he chuckles evilly.

"Well, don't just stand there. Get over here and wreck her pussy." He releases me, and I pull back, gasping for air.

"Oh, baby, you've never looked prettier," he says, stroking the side of my face. "Look at our mate, Nolan. Doesn't she look pretty?" He grabs my chin and turns me to face the furious man still standing in the doorway.

"Tell him, Glory, how much you want him to fill you with his seed. Shit, it is already full of three other mates' cum, so he might as well join the party. Maybe we'll end up with a baby."

His words make me pause for a moment. Fuck, I have been having a lot of unprotected sex. Shit, when was the last time I had a period? It was definitely before I met the guys. I try to count the weeks in my head, but before I can figure it all out, large hands grip my waist and drag me up. My eyes widen in surprise. I'd been so distracted by Mason's words, I hadn't kept an eye on Nolan.

He pushes down on my back. "Keep fucking her mouth," he growls as he yanks the hem of my dress up and around my waist.

I completely forget about my worries as he rips my panties off and shoves his cock deep with one thrust. I moan loudly, but it doesn't last, because Mason returns his dick to my mouth. They hold me between them and take turns thrusting in and out. My eyes roll back into my head as one of Nolan's meaty hands comes down and swats my ass.

"Fuck, you feel so good," he says with each thrust. "Hot and wet and full of our mates' cum. Going to make my own deposit and have you knocked up and round with our baby. Going to keep you that way with seven mates." My body tingles, and my nipples are painfully tight, as I slide one of my hands down to circle my clit. I'm so fucking close.

His words must be turning Mason on, because he's groaning as well. "Don't you come," Nolan barks at him. "You can fill our pussy too."

Holy fuck, all this dirty talk is too much, and white-hot ecstasy detonates through my body, my pussy pulsing around Nolan's fat cock. I choke on Mason's dick, unable to vocalize my pleasure, but that just seems to spur Nolan on.

"Fuck yeah, strangle my dick," he calls and slaps my ass, pounding harder and faster, pushing my orgasm to greater heights, before he stills and fills me with his cum, slowly swirling his dick around. "That's my good girl." He caresses the part of my ass he slapped, soothing away the sting as Mason pulls me forcefully off his dick, holding it at the base.

"Dude, you better hurry up, because I'm going to blow my load at any second."

I chuckle through my pleasure. My guys are so fucking romantic. Not.

"Fuck," Nolan grumbles but pulls out of me, and I feel his and the guys' combined releases leak out. "Brace your hands against the wall, Glory," he orders as he uses his fingers to shove his cum back in. "Get around here."

Mason quickly moves around and takes Nolan's place. I thought Nolan would go clean off, but instead, he slides underneath me and buries his head in my pussy, pushing my legs wide so he can lick my clit while Mason shoves his dick deep, our loud moans echoing through the bathroom.

Nolan laps at my clit as Mason slowly glides his cock in and out, building me to another exquisite peak.

"Oh fuck, Jesus Christ, Nolan," Mason mutters, our mate not being particularly careful with his tongue.

Nolan chuckles and flicks it across my clit again.

"Hurry up and get her there, man," Mason begs, sounding pained as Nolan latches his lips around my clit and sucks. My head hangs forward, and my legs wobble with the onslaught of pleasure. Mason swipes a finger around where he's currently sliding in out of my pussy, lubing it up before pushing it against my puckered asshole, sliding it into my ass and speeding up his thrusts.

It's enough to send me sailing into the stratosphere again, and this time, I can scream. Nolan wraps his arms around my legs, holding me steady as he flicks his tongue slowly over my overstimulated clit as Mason hammers hard before he, too, is coming.

"That pussy is going to be so full of our cum," Nolan mutters. "Going to keep it full of our cum as often as we can."

"Amen, brother." Mason runs a gentle hand

over my back but holds the other one out to Nolan for a high five. Nolan happily gives him one. Assholes.

Eventually, I have to tap Mason's thigh, pushing him away from me. I can't stay bent over any longer, and Nolan scrambles to his feet. They help me over to the shower, where Mason pulls my dress up and over my head before tossing it to the side so I can put it on again when we're done.

The two of them carefully wash me off, but they insist on shoving every bit of cum back into me. I'm too tired to think of the consequences at the moment, but future Glory really needs to think about when she last had her period.

Chapter Nine

I'm feeling pretty fucking amazing when we leave the changing rooms, all of us redressed and clean, although my hair is wet, but I dried it off as best as I could without access to a hair dryer like the last bathroom. I'm glad I kept the hair tie the hostess gave me, because I throw it up into a messy bun to keep the damp strands out of my face.

We find Carter, Louis, and Teddy all waiting for us near the elevators that lead to the other levels. There is another fight going on in the ring, and this time it's two women. I definitely want to come back to this club one day, but right now, I'd like to find Ben and Julian and get out of here.

"Hey, babe, great fight." Carter kisses Nolan on the lips before swinging his arm over me. "Did you take care of our hero?" he asks me.

"Of course I did."

"Yes, and I made a bundle." Mason approaches us from behind. He made a stop at the betting counter to cash in his winnings. My eyes widen as he carries a briefcase in each hand. "Idiots put him at high odds because it's been so long since he fought. We made a killing."

"Are they full of cash?" I ask him, and he nods.

"Sure are. A cool two million Hell dollars in each. Fancy fucking on a bed of cash when we get back to the palace?" He winks, and I giggle.

"That sounds like fun, but I don't really want to cover all our cash in cum. It might make it tricky to spend."

He tilts his head to the side and nods. "Good point. Maybe we will just make cash angels in it."

"What are we doing now?" Louis asks, waving at the buttons in front of us.

"Well, we need to chase down our last two mates," I suggest, feeling a little anxious now that they've been away for so long, especially since Ben is my newest bond and Julian isn't even bonded. I feel like I need to spend a little more time with each of them.

"Julian will be easy to find, so why don't you leave him until last? Ben is on the envy level, or that's where he said he was going. Tonight was drag queen runway or something, and as soon as he heard that, he was gone," Nolan tells me, leaning forward and pressing the button to call the car.

"How about we go up and wait in the bar Purgatory on the limbo level," Louis suggests, "while you find the other two? Then, we can all head back to the palace together. The car we brought is in the parking garage."

"Yeah, it's the only one. Every other spot had a Segway in it. It's so bizarre," Teddy grumbles. "Please tell me you're not going to go along with that stupid declaration about kangaroos. I would look ridiculous on a kangaroo."

"I guess we will have to wait and see," I tell him, and the doors open just in time so I can scurry in before he can grab me. I give them all a finger wave and hit the button for the envy level. "I'll see you all soon."

"Not too soon. Make sure you give your envy demon what he needs." Mason winks. "Alright, I guess the drinks are on me," he says to the guys as the doors close, leaving me in the elevator on my own. It's so nice to see them all getting along. I just need to make sure that Ben and Julian feel welcome and included. I don't doubt that those five won't make an effort, but I just want to keep a close eye on it all anyway.

Then there are the girls. Holy crap, how are they going to deal with all this? They like their lives, and they love school and daycare and hanging out with my mom and dads. Being confined to Hell is going to take some getting used to, but then if I am getting all of Lilith's powers, maybe I won't be confined to Hell—or at least I'm hoping the guys won't be.

The elevator stops on the envy level, and the doors open to a jaw-dropping sight. It looks like there's a brawl happening before my very eyes. Wigs, pasties, and shoes are flying as drag queens tackle one another, shouting obscenities and throwing punches. I'm a little scared to step out of the elevator and into the fray, but the doors try to close, so I have to suck it up and do it.

I stick close to the wall as I scan the brawl for my drag queen, but I can't see Poppy's flaming red hair anywhere. Then I remember the cubby space Ben showed me. The flaming red wig was certainly not the only one in there, so I scan the combatants, trying to find one that looks familiar. There, over in the corner, throwing a mighty right hook that wouldn't have been shameful in Nolan's fight, is Poppy. Today, she's wearing a long-haired black wig pulled up into a sleek ponytail with a bright purple mini dress, which is actually sitting at waist height at the moment, while she wrestles with another drag queen in a more Cinderella style ball gown in baby pink satin. I watch in horror as she lashes out, using her nails to scratch down Poppy's face.

"Hey, you bitch," I shout, wading through the fighting masses and pushing people out of my way to get to my prey. "Nobody marks up my girl but me." I get to them and grab the offending witch by the hand, and with a quick jerk of my own, I snap their wrist. She howls and snatches it back, cradling it against her chest.

"Who the fuck do you think you are?" she demands deeply, eyeing me up like she's trying to decide if she wants to have a go at me or not.

I pull my neckline to the side and show her the mark upon my chest. "I'm the next heir to Hell, and you're assaulting my mate."

She pales considerably and bows her head. "Fuck, I'm sorry. I had no idea. Please forgive me."

"Get out of here," I tell her, and she gets up and hurries away as security bursts into the room, dragging the rest of the fighters apart. I turn to face Poppy, looking her over, and she shimmies her dress down over her ass and rights herself. She either lost her hip padding in the brawl or decided to go without today, but her waist still tapers a little, giving her a sleek look, especially with the large breasts she's sporting. "Are you okay?" I ask her, and she blinks, looking like she's a little shocked, her long eyelashes fluttering.

"You defended me?" she says quietly.

"Yeah, of course I did. You're my mate. What did you think I would do, stand around and place bets?" I'm a little annoyed, not at her obviously, but at the fact that's how she expects to be treated because she doesn't know any differently.

She shakes her head, her long ponytail bobbing with the movement. "That's what Mabuz would have done." I place a finger over her mulberry stained lips.

"I don't want to hear that name cross your lips again, and I certainly don't want to hear you compare the two of us."

She pushes my finger away and throws her arms around my neck, pressing her lips to mine. I'm surprised but quickly wrap my own arms around her and kiss her back. It's a little weird having her breasts press against me, but I don't hate it. We're similar in height with me in heels and her not wearing any.

She walks me backward, oblivious to everything else that's going on around us. "That was so fucking hot," she says. "My dick is trying to bust out of its tape. Nobody has ever defended me like that before."

I find myself pressed up against a wall, with a door next to us saying, "Janitor." Poppy's hand, which slid down to grab a handful of my ass, reaches for the doorknob and pushes the door open, gently maneuvering me into the room and pulling the door closed behind us before locking it. Not once do our lips part, our tongues wrestling for dominance as I grab my own handful of ass to squeeze.

She pushes me back against a wall and lifts me, allowing me to wrap my legs around her waist. I try to grind against her, but I pout with disappointment when there's nothing to grind on.

She chuckles. "Hang on." She drops me back to my feet, hikes up her dress, reaches between her legs, and does something to un-tape her dick. She sighs with relief and throws the tape to the side. "Being strapped is no fun with a boner."

Poppy lifts me up again and pushes me against the wall, taking my mouth with hers. This time when I grind, I get exactly what I need, and both of us groan.

"God, I love you," Poppy says against my mouth, her hand creeping up to caress my breast. "And I love your breasts. I'm so freaking jealous, sometimes I wish I had breasts too." She leans down and rubs her face against them, practically purring with delight.

I put my hands on her cheeks and lift her head so I'm looking her in the eye. "Really?" I ask, and she purses her lips and shrugs.

"Sure, I'm an envy demon. On days when I want to be Poppy, it would be nice to have the real thing."

"Permanently?" I ask, and she lifts her eyes in thought but quickly shakes her head.

"Nah, I like being Ben too, but a set of breasts like this when I'm Poppy would make all the other queens green with envy."

"I may be able to help you with that after I'm

crowned," I tell her. Hell, if Lilith can create Hell kangaroos from nothing, and I can kill Mabuz with a thought, then surely I can give Poppy boobs whenever she wants.

Her pretty mouth drops open with surprise as her eyes widen. "You could do that for me?"

"Fuck yeah. We want you to win as many pageants and shows as you desire," I tell her. "And, I mean, it might be fun for you to have tits when we fuck, then I could play with yours too." I reach out and give her pasties a squeeze, winking so she knows I want to give her everything within my capacity to give.

She growls and reaches down, tearing my panties from my body, and I shiver at the intense desire in her eyes. "I'm going to fuck you so hard now. You're never going to be sad that I'm your mate."

"Oh, baby, I never would be," I assure her, that poor, insecure soul shining through her eyes.

She reaches down and pulls her cock out of her own panties before impaling me hard. She groans, and her eyes roll back as my own moan fills the small room.

"Oh fuck, you've been playing with all your other mates. I can feel them. You're so hot and full of cum in there." She slowly slides out before rolling her hips and sliding back in.

"Yeah, Carter and Louis fucked me on the gluttony level surrounded by cake and filled my pussy and ass," I tell her, my words shaky as she lazily slides in and out, slowly building us to exquisite peaks.

"Oh, that sounds like fun. I want to do that too." She nudges the top of my dress down with her nose, exposing my breasts.

"Tell me more," she begs before taking one of my nipples into her mouth and lavishing it with attention.

"Well, then Teddy fucked me in the arena while we watched Nolan's fight."

She stops what she's doing and lifts her head, her eyes wide with shock. "In front of everyone?"

"Yeah, I mean, we were covered with a blanket, but I rode his cock and cheered for Nolan. It was fucking hot."

"Ugh, fuck, that made my balls tingle. Tell me more," she begs as she speeds up her thrusts, her long dick filling me with every smooth stroke.

I reach out and wind my arms around her neck then run my tongue across my lips. She follows the movement with her eyes, captivated by everything I'm telling her.

"Then I sucked Mason's cock in the changing room while we waited for Nolan, and then they spit roasted me before both of them filled me with their cum." I kiss her and then pull back. "Can you taste Mason's cock when you're kissing me?" I ask the dirty question, and even though he didn't come in my mouth, it's still fun to tease her.

"No, but I wish I could," she admits, looking me dead in the eye.

"Oh, I'm sure you'll get a chance," I assure her. "We are all going to have so much fun together." If our life span is anything like Luc's, then we have many, many years to do it.

Poppy's thrusts pick up, her hands squeezing my ass tight where she holds me against the wall. My head falls back against the wall, lifting my breasts, and she sucks and nibbles them. She bends her knees and powers into me, going deeper than before, and my breath hitches before a keening sound comes from my mouth.

Pinning me against the wall with her body, she slips a hand around to tease my clit, igniting every sensitive part in my body.

"More, please," I rasp out as she pounds into me, burying her head in my shoulder.

"So close," she mutters and increases the speed on my clit, my pussy clenching around her long length, and both of us moan. When her head lifts, the love and affection I see in her eyes makes my heart and soul clench, and I splinter into a thousand pieces, the pleasure tearing through my limbs indescribable.

"God, Glory," she moans as my core ripples around her length, making her movements jerky and uneven until she, too, stills, adding her cum to the loads that I've already been filled with today. "Love you," she mutters as my hands explore the muscles on her back, my pleasure spiking and then ebbing like gentle waves on a shore.

"Love you too." I take her lips and kiss her like I'll never get a chance to kiss her again. It's hard and fierce as I use my teeth to nip her lips, biting just a little harder than normal so I can leave my mark on her.

She gasps and runs her tongue over her lip, feeling the blood welling there. "I like to mark what's mine," I tell her so she never has any doubt about how I feel.

Her confusion fades away, and her lips stretch into a blinding smile, and I know I said the right thing. It might take a while, because she obviously has some deep-seated issues, but I will make sure to let her know each and every day that she is loved, accepted, and wanted.

Chapter Ten

"What the hell happened? What started that brawl?" I ask Poppy once she sets me down.

"Fucking crazy bitches," she says, her eyes comically wide. "It was the talent portion of the contest, and I announced I was going to sing Taylor Swift's 'Cruel Summer' as my piece. I thought nobody would know it here because it's a recent Earth song. It takes a while for things to travel to this plane. Well, I was so surprised, you could have smeared me with butter and called me a biscuit, but at least five others also wanted to perform the same song."

I feel my brow wrinkle as I try to puzzle out everything she just told me, getting stuck on the smearing her with butter and calling her a biscuit. "What?"

"And that's when the fight started. One of the girls pushed another one out of her way by her falsies, and she stumbled on her ridiculously high heels and fell into me, knocking me into the gal on the other side of me, then it was on." She looks at me with complete and utter love in her eyes. "I was holding my own until that bitch used her nails to scratch my face. She caught me across the eye, and I couldn't see through the tears."

I run a finger over the very distinct welts running down the left side of her face. It looks like they may have drawn a little blood, and whatever residual guilt I felt for snapping her wrist dissipates.

She reaches out and pulls my own dress down. My panties are long gone, but she quickly mutters the magic spell and pulls a pair of briefs out of her interdimensional space for me. "I can't imagine it's fun walking with cum sliding down the inside of your thighs." She giggles. "And there was already quite a bit in there. It felt like you had a very fun night."

I reach out and use both hands to straighten her breasts under her dress. Somehow, our frantic movements pushed them out of alignment. It probably didn't help that I kept grabbing onto them.

"I did, but I'm starving again, and I still haven't found Julian."

"Well, you're in luck. The sloth level will bring snacks to you in bed, so you don't actually have to move. Shall we go find him? We can have a little rest and maybe get some food into you as well."

"You don't need to stay and finish the competition?" I ask her as she unlocks the door and peers out before shaking her head.

"Nope, looks like everyone was sent home. There's a hell of a mess to clean up in there. Come on, let's get out of here." She takes my hand and drags me across the room littered with various different drag queen paraphernalia. There are a couple of annoyed janitorial staff cleaning it all up, but all the other contestants and audience members have been cleared out.

"You know, I'd love to see you perform that song one day," I tell Poppy as we approach the elevator, and she presses the button. She turns to face me, her gorgeous gray eyes wide with shock.

"You would?" she asks hesitantly.

"Of course, baby. I want whatever makes you happy. I'm sure the girls would love it too. They are big Tay-Tay fans. Maybe we should see if we can get you and the girls tickets to her next concert."

Poppy claps her hands and jumps up and down on the spot. "Oh my god. That would be amazing. I've never been to a concert or show before apart from my own of course."

"Not even before you went to Earth? Do they have that sort of thing here in Hell?"

"No, I was a foster kid, remember? No one has spare money to take us to things like that. And yes, Luc regularly brings rock stars to Hell and then either implants another memory or mind wipes them. You know when an artist cancels a concert at the last minute unexpectedly? That's usually Luc, or someone he sent, of course."

She steps into the elevator, but my steps grind to a halt. "Is that the kind of thing I'm going to have to do now?" I ask, and she beams.

"Sure is, honey, but don't worry, I got a whole list of acts and shows I want to see here in Hell. Maybe I could be your entertainment minister or something." She waves me in, and I follow automatically, then she presses the button for the sloth level.

"Holy shit, Poppy. You are a freaking genius. I bet Mason would be awesome as my minister of finance, and Nolan as minister of defense." I'm on a roll now, but I stop.

"Do we need a minister of defense? Is there anything we need to defend against?" She taps a manicured finger against one cheek. Holy crap, where did that come from? She didn't have those earlier. They must be press on. "Actually, I don't know. There's always been rumors about angels wanting to invade, but how true that is, I'm not sure."

"Okay, well, when everything settles down a bit, we need to work all of this out." I pace back and forth across the small box, and Poppy watches on. I didn't think about how much was involved in running a whole entire plane of existence until she said those things.

"Aww, Glory, don't be nervous. Luc has a whole council of people to help him, and you can too. Trust me, you are going to be amazing at this because you love and care so hard." Poppy stops me from walking and puts her hand against my cheek. "You're amazing, and I have never felt so wanted and seen in my whole life." She rubs her nose against mine as the elevator pings, letting us know we've arrived. "Come on, let me feed you." She tugs me out of the elevator and into another foyer.

"Fuck, I don't have any money. I left my cards at home. I'm such an idiot."

"Don't worry, I was worried about the same thing, I don't have any money either. I've been kept by Mabuz all this time, and he took any money I earned at the show, but Carter started an account here and added us all to it and told me not to worry." She blushes a little. "Your mates are wonderful."

A wide smile stretches across my face. "They are your mates too, so go get yourself some of that if you want." I hip bump her, and she blushes even brighter.

"Maybe one day, but for now, I want to enjoy what you and I have."

Fuck, my beating heart skips, and it's my turn to blush.

"Can I help you?" A hostess wearing a slinky nightgown approaches.

"Yes, can you please show us to Julian Beamus's pod please?" I say pleasantly, still high on my orgasm and Poppy, but she raises a skeptical eyebrow, eyeballing us like we're requesting something shocking, and my high quickly fades away.

"The gatekeeper asked not to be disturbed. We don't allow groupies to stalk our clients."

"Excuse me, bitch." Poppy puffs up her chest and goes to step forward, but I put out a hand, stroking her arm to calm her.

"I'm sure he appreciates your dedication to your job, but if you could tell him his mates are here to join him, I would appreciate it," I state firmly, and she scoffs and looks down her hawk beak nose at me.

"Pfft, you two are his mates?" The derision is familiar and exactly the same tone that Jenny and Nicole gave me when they found out I was mated to Nolan.

"Oh, sweetheart, I would stop while you're ahead. You have no idea who you are talking to," Poppy says in a singsong tone behind me as I see red. I am sick to death of uppity little bitches making assumptions from appearances. Sure, I've been fucked six ways to Sunday, literally, and showered twice since I left the palace. I admit I am not at my absolute best, but how dare this little lazy ass sloth demon who probably does nothing but lie around all day pass judgment on me. I am a mate, a mother, and I also manage to run a successful food blog as well as training to become a bounty hunter. I am nothing to be sneered at, and she has gotten on my very last nerve.

"Listen here, bitch," I snarl, and the girl steps back a little.

"Security," she shouts shrilly, and two men appear out of nowhere and grab my arms. "Remove this trash from the club."

"Unhand me," I growl, but neither of them listen, and they try to drag me away as Poppy swats at them.

A deep, thunderous growl echoes through the room, making them freeze. From out of the dark depths of the hallway leading away from the foyer steps an animal so fearsome, it's enough to make a grown man shit his pants. Cerberus's eyes glow lavender with fury, and all three muzzles are growling.

"Take your hands off our mate immediately," the middle head demands, and the two guards quickly release me like I'm poisonous to the touch before backing away very swiftly.

"How dare you treat our mate this way. Be gone, and make sure you are never in our presence again," the right head growls. The two guards scurry away, the left head snapping at their heels, but the hostess stands her ground and pulls down on the hem of her damn nighty, almost exposing her nipples.

"Apologies, guardian, but these two claimed they are your mates. Surely that's not true," she prattles, fluttering her eyelashes at him.

Sometimes I really hate the female species, despite being one.

"Are you deaf as well as dumb?" the left head sneers at her. "Did you not hear our declaration?"

"Well, I mean, look at them." She waves a hand in our direction, but I happen to think Poppy and I look quite good considering we were in a fight and then fucked like mad not twenty minutes ago. We tidied up nicely.

"You dare insult Hell's heir?" the middle head thunders loudly, and the woman gasps as I pull down the edge of my dress again to show my mark.

"Her?" The woman sounds incredulous.

"Oh fuck, just eat her now, Cerberus, and be done with it. Bitch doesn't know when to quit," Poppy says to our mate, who doesn't hesitate to do as she suggested. Instead of eating her, though, the three heads open their mouths and blow out streams of fire, and the woman's screams cut off as she turns to ash.

I stare, blinking for a moment, my nose wrinkling up at the smell of burnt flesh. "Well, shit, that escalated quickly."

"Not quickly enough." The middle head glares

at the pile of ash before spitting on it. Huh, I didn't know dogs could spit. "As the ruler of Hell, you need to be swift with your justice. Do not allow anyone to spout shade on your rule. You'll rule for a long time, and we do not want anyone getting delusions of grandeur."

"Yup, you do not want another Mabuz," Poppy chimes in, studying her fingernails. "Shoot, one of these popped off during the fight. I hate it when my nails look all raggedy."

"Fight? What fight?" The right head pins us with a narrow-eyed glare.

"Cool your jets, puppy." Poppy saunters over and gives each of them a pat on the head. "Our girl took care of it. Now she's hungry and could probably use some snuggles, so how about you lead us back to Julian's pod and let him make a reappearance."

Poppy is so much more assertive than Ben. I hope they both come to realize that they never have to be afraid to be assertive and tell us what they want.

All three of Cerberus's heads huff before they start to shimmer and Julian stands there in all his naked glory. Poppy is not shy and takes a long look at our mate's naked body, and I won't even lie and say I shifted my gaze. Nope, I take in all he has to work with, and wow, it is something impressive. Julian's body is more like Poppy's than the rest of them. He's slender and lean, with some muscle definition. I guess that makes sense, with him being a sloth demon. Working out would be the last thing on his mind.

It's Poppy's pursed lips and raised eyebrows that have me looking lower to where she's staring.

"What is that?" The words hiss out of me, and I point to the base of his cock.

Julian smirks, and his eyes twinkle. "When Cerberus and I merged, he got a bit of my humanity and, well, I got a fancy new cock."

"Is that what I think it is?" Poppy asks, tapping a finger against her cheek and leaning down a bit to get a better look. Julian's cock starts to swell from all the attention.

"If you think it is a knot, then yes indeed."

"A knot? You mean, like a dog? Like shifters in a freaking paranormal romance novel?" I ask, unable to hide the surprise in my voice.

"You bet it is." He sounds smug as fuck. "The ladies and men love it. It makes fucking extra fun. We lock together, and my knot swells and vibrates on the G-spot or prostate. Makes orgasms super intense for everyone." At the mention of past conquests, I start to see red, and my temper boils, and I growl.

Poppy stands up and shakes her head, backing away from Julian. "Oh no, man, that was not the right thing to say. You won't be getting your knot wet again at all."

"I am fucking fed up with all the man whores my mates have been," I seethe through gritted teeth. "Why do you think I want to hear about all the people you've previously fucked, or how much they liked that knot? Do I go bragging to you about all the men I fucked before meeting Nolan? Should I tell you about the boyfriend who liked to spank me and have me call him Daddy? Or the one who had a piercing in his cock that used to hit me in just the right spot? Or what about the one who would finger fuck me so good, I would squirt?"

The smirk drops, and his face grows darker with every comment I make until he's growling much like Cerberus.

"See? It's not so fun, is it? So how about you shut your pie hole if you ever want to stick it in anything ever again?"

I storm off down the darkened hallway he appeared from, leaving behind the pile of hostess ash for someone else to clean up. There doesn't seem to be anyone else around for the moment. Instead of waiting for Julian to show us where his pod is, I just go in search of one of my own. Fuck him.

The low lighting shows me that the pods differ in size, from what seems like maybe a single-sized bed right up to an Alaskan king. I pick one some-where in between, conscious of wanting space for Poppy too. I kick off my shoes and climb up on the cloud-like mattress, sighing with pleasure as my body sinks into the softness. I can hear Poppy and Julian following closely behind me, muttering quietly to one another. As mad as I am at Julian, I hope he and Poppy strike up a friendship. I don't want either of them to feel left out, and with the rest of the group dynamics, it's quite possible that they will.

I roll over onto my side, my back to the opening of the pod, and think about how I just reacted. Why was I so fucking mad about what he said? Is it because he's my last mate and still not bonded to me, or does it have something to do with the mate challenge? I know he said he couldn't stand Imogen, but there's a good chance he probably dipped his dick in that crazy before he discovered the actual crazy. Does she know what that knot feels like? Or does it have nothing to do with that and everything to do with wanting to be the heir to Hell?

"Glory," Poppy says softly, interrupting my thoughts, "can we join you?"

I huff and roll to face them, avoiding looking at Julian. "Yes, come on in." Poppy quickly climbs in and snuggles into my side, while Julian stays where he is, eyeing me warily.

I gesture him forward with my head. "Come on,

I'm sorry I lost my shit. I think maybe the stress of everything is getting to me."

He shakes his head, his eyes sorrowful. "No, sorry, that was my fault. I'm feeling a little insecure, and I let my ego get the better of me. I shouldn't have explained it like I did. Please forgive me."

"Well done, you two. This is all going to take a lot of communication and understanding, and apologizing when we know we were wrong is a great start." Poppy pats the side of the bed, but Julian hesitates, and her face falls at the rejection. I decide I may very well smite this man, but before I can say anything, she does. "I mean, I can move onto Glory's other side if you don't want to snuggle into me."

Julian frowns and shakes his head vigorously. "No, that's not what I meant, you're very sexy. I'd be more than happy to snuggle with you, but I was worried it might upset Glory because we aren't bonded yet.

And there he goes, being sweet and making up for his previous behavior, and I can tell by the way Poppy practically swoons that she agrees.

"Get into the bed, Julian. We are all mates, so I am not going to be jealous if you snuggle with Poppy." He climbs up onto the bed, eases down next to my envy mate, and gently wraps his arms around her waist, then he snuggles in big spoon style. The frown drops, and a large sigh of relief leaves his mouth.

"Hmm, this is nice," he says as his eyes start to drift closed. Poppy giggles but looks ecstatic and wiggles like a puppy with excitement. It's so cute.

"Settle, Gretel, you can't go to sleep until you show me how to order some food to the bed. A big greasy pizza will go a long way in keeping me happy. I've done a fair amount of exercise tonight, and I'm starving."

"Exercise? What the Hell have you been doing?" Julian asks, and Poppy giggles.

"Had her brains fucked out by all of her mates but you."

Julian groans, his head falling forward into Poppy's neck. "Ugh, now I'm thinking about watching that, and I'm getting a boner." He nuzzles her neck, and I watch with amusement as he grinds said boner against her ass, and she moans. "Sorry."

"Food for me first, and then if you two want to fuck, I won't be upset with dinner and a show."

Chapter Eleven

Julian orders me a veritable feast, and while I eat it, the two of them make out a little but don't go any further. Julian wants to be officially bonded to me before he messes around with anyone else, and I respect that. By the time I'm done, I'm horny and happy and ready to head home to sleep it all off.

"I could get used to this club," I tell my two mates as we get into the elevator.

"That's good, considering you own it." Julian chuckles as he pushes the button to take us up to the limbo level.

"Excuse me?" I stammer as both my and Poppy's mouths drop open.

"Seven Circles is owned by the crown. You are free to use it whenever you want. Luc has his private pod on the sloth level and various different arrangements on all the others. I'm sure once your existence becomes common knowledge, everyone will quickly start kissing your ass. You won't get any other shade thrown at you like that hostess."

I wrinkle my nose. "Are we going to get into trouble for that?" I ask, and Julian scoffs.

"Fuck no. It's part of my job to protect the ruler and, by extension, that means you. You are going to have to be swift and harsh with your punishments in the coming weeks so that people don't assume you're going to be a pushover and challenge you for your rule."

"I'm not sure I can do that," I tell him as the doors open behind us, allowing us to step out into a crowded bar area.

"You're lucky you have me then. I doubt any of the other guys are going to let anyone hurt you either."

Julian stops and peers around the room, spotting our mates across the crowd. Instead of dragging us through the tables to our mates, he gestures to tell them we are leaving. All five of them quickly drain their drinks and get up from the table they are at. I watch with amusement as they walk through the crowded bar. Occasionally, people try to start up a conversation, but they are all shaken off or ignored. There are many pouting faces left in their wake, it makes me smile. I can see what a fucking handsome group of men they are, and I don't blame people for trying, but I also feel smug that they are all mine.

"Oh." Poppy shivers next to me. "The envy in here is fucking delicious. I feel like I could take over the world." She rubs her arms, and I can see the hair on them standing up like it's statically charged.

"Hey, you look tired but happy," Carter says as they reach me, each of them giving me a kiss on the lips.

"I am so ready for bed, but we also need to work out a strategy for tomorrow's challenge," I tell them, my heart sinking. I can't believe I still have to deal with that.

"Hey, baby, we've got you," Mason says, putting his arm around Teddy. "The five of us have a plan. We just have to fill you in. Trust us?"

"Yeah, of course," I reply, and they all grin.

"Come on, let's head back to the palace and get a good night's sleep. We can go over it all in the morning." Louis grabs my hand and drags me into the foyer through a side door. From there, the seven of them escort me out to the parking lot and the waiting limo. The driver is sitting in the front seat, reading a book, but he puts it aside as we climb in.

"The palace please," Julian says politely, and the driver nods and waits for us all to be seated before pulling out of the parking lot, careful not to hit any of the Segways.

"I am so bringing back cars," I mutter, not ever wanting to get on one of those wretched things again.

"I'm sure you won't hear any complaints from the denizens of Hell." Julian smiles, leaning back and closing his eyes. Funnily enough, Nolan does the same thing and rests his head on Julian's shoulder. Julian's eyes snap open, and he looks down at him, startled, but Nolan just ignores him, so Julian shrugs and closes his eyes again. I guess they really did work out their issues.

The trip back only takes about half an hour, but that's long enough for everyone in the car except Poppy and I to fall asleep. I guess I did wear them all out. Poppy giggles and spends the trip picking off the rest of her false nails and putting them in the little trash bin. She holds them up when she's done.

"That looks better. I hate it when they are uneven," she tells me. She looks down at her feet. Her toenails are painted bright red, and she screws up her nose. "I can't believe I lost my shoes. They were a gorgeous pair of black Prada pumps that Mabuz gifted me. I bet one of those bitches saw them and stole them after the fight."

"Don't worry. When things settle, you can go back to Earth and get yourself another pair or two. After all, if you're going to be my entertainment minister, you're going to need to look the part. Maybe you can grab a few nice pairs for Ben too."

She bounces up and down in her seat, and I get a rush of warmth. I kind of like feeling like a sugar mama and want to spoil this person so badly to make up for how shitty their life has been.

When we get to our wing of the palace, everyone goes their separate ways. The room I'm in doesn't have a bed big enough for all of us, and it seems like an unspoken consensus from the other five to leave me alone with Poppy and Julian for now. How sweet are they, trying to make sure that my two newest mates are secure in their place? None of them leave, though, without kissing me silly. I'm panting and flushed by the time I join Julian in our assigned room.

"Where's Poppy?" I ask, looking around, and he points to the bathroom door. "Cool. I showered twice tonight, so I don't think I need another one," I tell him, pulling out a tank to wear to bed. I'm officially keeping the briefs Poppy gave me because they are comfy as fuck and don't creep up my ass at all. "I just want to brush my teeth and pee before we go to bed."

"Do you want me to shift into Cerberus and sleep on the floor?" Julian asks, and I turn and face him, surprised by his question.

"No, why?" I ask him, and I see a little insecurity on his face.

"Well, we haven't bonded yet and…" He trails off, and I roll my eyes.

"Stop it, of course I want you on the bed, and I don't care who you want to sleep next to. If the two of you want to create a Glory sandwich, I'm good with that. If you're not ready to sleep next to me, we can sandwich Poppy."

The door opens, and Ben steps out, freshly cleaned of makeup and eyelashes and rubbing his hair with a towel. There's also one wrapped around his waist. Both Julian and I watch a droplet of water trail down his chest, and he smirks.

"I vote we sandwich Glory between us. Just because you can't seal your bond until after the challenge doesn't mean the two of you shouldn't get to know one another." He's got a wicked gleam in his eye.

"Well, actually, you know any kind of sexual contact can trigger the bond, and if we do that before the challenge tomorrow, and Glory loses for some reason, then we all die." Julian's tone is solemn, and Ben's grin drops.

"Shit no, let's not do that then, but we can still snuggle. You can tell us about your hobbies and things you like to do."

Julian scoffs as I push past him and enter the bathroom to brush my teeth and use the toilet. "I'm a sloth demon, I like to sleep and game. Anything that doesn't involve actual work."

I do what I have to do and can hear the two of them chatting quietly, and when I return to the main bedroom, I find them both in bed with a gap between them large enough for me.

"Come on." Ben pats the space and grins. "Julian and I were just talking about video games. There wasn't a lot for me to do in my downtime in Mabuz's compound, so I became proficient at them too. We're going to find a console and play once the whole challenge and crowning are over with."

"Aww, look at the two of you bonding." I climb up and crawl across the bed, and both of their gazes lock onto the cleavage I'm rocking in my tank top. I giggle, delighted at their reactions. I'm woman enough to admit it's nice to be admired like I'm the last cupcake on a plate.

I maneuver myself under the covers, my ass brushing briefly across Julian's face, and he groans quietly before muttering, "Fuck, talk about an exercise in restraint."

I snuggle down between them, and they both crowd in close, their legs against mine providing a stark contrast. Ben's are smooth and silky, whereas Julian's are lightly covered in hair and tickle my own.

"Thank you, Glory," Ben whispers, pressing a kiss to my cheek as my eyes drift closed. "I love being mated to you."

"And I can't wait to be mated to you. The minute you finish that challenge, I'm going to bend you over and show you what my knot really feels like," Julian mutters, and Ben scoffs.

"Dude, you're so romantic."

"Fuck, if she wants romance, she has the French fuck for that. I'm going to give her a religious experience and have her seeing Jesus."

"Wait." I sit up quickly, and they huff with disappointment. "Is Jesus real?" I ask, looking at my sloth mate who rolls his eyes and pulls me back down on the bed.

"Yes, he's one of those stuffy angels and the reason why angels aren't allowed on Earth anymore. He stirred up religious fervor, and God basically dragged them all back to Heaven when the humans crucified him. He was scared that his perfectly pious angels would rebel."

"God left him there?" Ben sounds horrified, and Julian's disgust is evident.

"Yes, as a learning lesson to all the other angels. He could have rescued him. He wouldn't have died from his original injuries, but he chose to make a statement."

"What a douche," I say as I settle back down. "I hope I never meet him."

"Yeah, you're not going to be able to avoid him. Luc and God regularly have handovers. Well, I mean, God tosses the angels he deems unworthy out, and Luc accepts them with open arms. Barbs are thrown and meltdowns occur, mostly God's. It's fun and games all around." Julian leans in and kisses me on the cheek, his touch lingering, and when I turn to look at him, the sheer want in his eyes is breath stealing. "But don't worry, I'll be by your side, and Cerberus scares the poop out of him. He hates dogs. He's a cat person."

With that information imparted, my sloth demon starts snoring soundly, all snuggled up to my side.

"Fuck me," Ben hisses. "We're going to have to face God? Is it too late to return to Earth and pretend that mark never appeared?" He snuggles closer, and I run my hand through his hair in a soothing gesture. "We can just go back to normal, everyday, boring, nonlethal life."

"I don't think there's much chance of that now. Even if we managed to get through the portal, Luc would send people after me. That's even if Julian could leave. No, we just need to suck it up and work on a plan. If I even have an inkling of what my uncle is like, I bet he knows ways to stir God up by just breathing. We'll make sure we have our own tricks up our sleeves."

"I can't believe your grandpa is God," he says, pressing against my hand in his hair, practically purring with delight. Julian snuffles quietly in his sleep next to us. His face is all relaxed in his slumber and has a boyish quality to it much like Ben's does.

"Wait until you meet my grandma," I tell him, rolling over and scooping him into my arms, making him my little spoon. He sighs with contentment, and soon enough, his breathing evens out and he's asleep too.

So much information is rolling around in my head. Everything I've learned today and everything that has happened should be keeping me awake, but I trust my guys have a plan in place and will let me know tomorrow. For now, I'm just going to let it all go and sleep.

The next morning, we are up bright and early and have a feast awaiting us when we all convene in the dining hall. Unlike the mass of guests last night, it's my mates minus Nolan, Luc, and his two lieutenants at breakfast, and the table is round so we can all see each other. Luc has dark circles under his eyes and doesn't look like he slept well at all.

"Are you okay?" I ask him, and he smiles ruefully, downing a large sip of coffee.

"Yeah, just eager to go after my mate. Each time she returns to Hell, it gets harder and harder for me to function with a clear mind."

"You know for sure she is your mate?" I ask, sounding skeptical. Kerry wasn't sure at all.

"Yes, I knew the minute I held her in my arms

when she was a babe that she was my mate." He holds out his hand, it is circled by the colored bands. Yellow, red, and green. Greed, wrath, and envy.

"But she doesn't have a colored ring," I argue.

"No, colored rings only appear after a demon achieves their majority. Kerry was just a babe the last time they touched, and as such, she hasn't gotten a ring yet," Leviathan explains, squeezing Luc's shoulder in comfort.

"But it won't be long. As soon as that crown is on your head, we are blowing this joint," Beelzebub growls and rubs his hands together. "There is no place on Earth that girl can hide where we won't find her."

"Speaking of which, Mason approached me before you arrived. He would like me to teleport you out of the arena and to wherever Julian is the minute you beat Imogen so that no one has a chance to challenge you before you seal your bond with him. Are you okay with that?"

I nod. "Absolutely. I've been chosen for a reason, and I want to be the best ruler Hell has ever had," I say solemnly, and Luc frowns.

"But I'm the only ruler Hell has had."

"Exactly," I tell him but can't keep a straight face, and I wink before giggling.

He growls as everyone else around us laughs, including his two mates.

Nolan appears through a side door, coming over and giving me a kiss on the cheek. "The girls are fine," he tells me. He stayed behind to call his parents. He wanted to check on the girls and make sure they hadn't seen the challenge announcement. He didn't want them to worry. "Mom and Dad made sure they didn't see the announcements. Dad says to kick her ass." He grabs my hand and squeezes it tightly. "The girls said to give you all big hugs and kisses. You can't lose this, Glory. My girls wouldn't recover."

I squeeze his hand back, tears prickling in my eyes. "I won't let them down," I promise, my stomach rolling, hoping I can keep that promise.

"So what's the plan for Imogen?" Luc asks, and I wince.

"Um, we haven't gotten as far as discussing it."

"What?" he shouts, and I shrug.

"Well, we were a little busy last night," I tell him, and all of my mates chuckle or smirk, and I roll my eyes.

"It's simple." Mason leans forward, grinning. "You're going to Indiana Jones her."

"Huh?" Leviathan looks confused, and so does Beelzebub, and I can safely say I am with them, but Luc is grinning and claps his hands with joy.

"Bravo, I like it, she will never see it coming."

"Can you share with the rest of us?" I ask, pointing at the two lieutenants and myself.

"So you tell them you choose weapons. Imogen will pull out her swords and wave them around, probably taunting you to frustrate you and make you clumsy, but then you reach into your interdimensional space, pull out a gun, and shoot her between her eyes. It's the whole she brought a knife to a gun fight thing." He leans back and crosses his arms, smug as can be, and I can practically see my mates patting themselves on their metaphorical backs.

Oh okay, now I am with them. I remember that part in the movie. Are they freaking stupid? "The problem is that Indie's opponent didn't have wings," I tell them through gritted teeth. How can they forget something so vital?

"Please, we have seen you hit a moving target. You will be fine." Nolan waves off my concern, and I want to throttle him.

I might be able to help with that. Lilith's voice echoes inside my head before her ghostly apparition appears, floating above the table, causing all of my men to shriek and tumble out of their chairs.

"Have I said how much I love my granny?" I say out loud, smirking at them and thinking they really deserve it this morning after the crap they just pulled. Do they want me to die?

Chapter Twelve

"Lilith, what are you doing?" Luc hisses, standing up and glaring at his mother.

"What, darling? I thought I might come and have breakfast with you, and meet all of Glory's gorgeous mates." She looks around the table, shooting them flirty winks and blowing them kisses. I giggle, but Luc huffs an annoyed sound.

He waves a hand, and an opaque, shimmery dome surrounds the table, blocking us from view of anyone who may peer into the dining hall.

"Damn it, woman. You know what would happen if it became common knowledge that you are here. Mabuz might catch wind of it and try the draining spell in that book. We can't let that happen until all power has been transferred to Glory."

"Which is going to happen as soon as she beats that ingrate of a grandchild and then rides Julian like a pony. Relax, everything will be fine." My grandmother nods at my final mate, brushing off Luc's concerns. He grits his teeth so hard and growls, I'm worried he's going to break something. "Glory can't go into that fight at a disadvantage, so I'm just going to even the playing field. She is, after all, of our bloodline."

With that vague comment, and without going into any other details, Lilith drifts toward me. "Stand up, dear, and come over here," she says, and I do as she requests.

I watch as her incorporeal form drifts behind me, and then there's a searing pain, like she's shoved her hands into my back. I cry out, and my knees buckle, but I'm held in place. I can hear my mates shouting and trying to get to me, but Luc waves a hand and holds them in place.

"Be patient," he tells them, obviously in the know.

My breath heaves in and out as tears flow down my face. It feels like Lilith is trying to rearrange my insides. She mutters to herself at the same time.

"Nearly there. Ah, got them." With that, it feels like she pulls her hands out. There's a whooshing sound, and the complaints from my mates stop in an instant as they look behind me.

"Holy fuck," Teddy mutters, his eyes wide.

"What the hell? Hers are prettier than mine," Luc complains, collapsing back in his chair and pouting like a toddler.

There's a weight on my back that wasn't there before, and when I move, I hear the rustle of feathers. I try to turn my head, but I can't see what they are all staring at, though I think I have an idea.

"There, now you and Imogen will have a fair fight," Lilith says, and a full-length mirror appears in front of me. I gape at my reflection. Behind me, attached to my back, are beautiful feathery wings. Unlike Luc's, which are white with threads of red and gold, mine are blood-red with threads of silver.

"But isn't she at a disadvantage now? How is she going to be able to learn to use them in time?" Ben sounds devastated as he points out a perfectly rational issue.

"Pfft." Lilith waves her hand at him. "Like I wouldn't plant the innate knowledge in her brain on how to use them. Give it a try, it will be like you were born with them."

I look around the room, and my mates appear worried, but what else can I do but trust her? I think about bringing them forward so I can touch them, and sure enough, my wings curve forward in front of me, almost cocooning my body, and I reach out and stroke the feathers. They are silky smooth and pillowy soft. I am not sure how they are going to be able to hold me aloft.

As I think about flying, they snap out, and I brace myself to lift, but I go nowhere. I look around the room, and everyone else looks as confused as I do except Luc.

"You have to push off with your knees, a small

jump, and then you will move," he tells me, glaring at his mother.

"Whoops, forgot that bit," she says, and her apparition looks like it blushes slightly, which is weird because she doesn't have any blood. It must be a reflex.

I bend my knees and jump, and sure enough, I lift into the air, my wings flapping behind me. Lilith is right. Once I'm up here, I know instinctively what I have to do. We are still enclosed by the opaque dome, so I let myself drift back to the ground.

"Wow." I can't help but grin like a loon because that was amazing, but there is a small ache in my back, and I roll my shoulders to try and ease it.

"You'll hurt for a while until you build up the muscles that are necessary to use them." Luc scowls at his mom. "That's why it wasn't ideal to yank them out like that."

"Does my mom have wings?" I ask, and both he and his mom nod.

"Yes, but she probably hasn't used them since she left Hell. A big, flying angel in the sky is pretty hard to hide," Luc replies.

Yeah, I guess he's right. "What happens if I shoot Imogen in the wings? Will that stop her from flying?" I ask, and Luc shakes his head.

"No. Although they feel soft, a bullet will bounce off them. They are nearly impenetrable except by a special weapon made in Heaven infused with God's power. Only a select few were given one of those, and three of them no longer reside in there. Only my brother and God have access to that weapon, and neither of them would give their sword to Imogen, even if she is a plant. They use them to remove the wings of angels bound for Hell."

"When you said they lost their wings…" I trail off, not even wanting to speak out loud about the horror.

"Yes, God cut their wings from their backs. Any of the original demons from Heaven will have scars. All demons born here have been born without them and no scars."

"That's fucking barbaric," I say as my wings flutter with agitation behind me. Now that I have them, I feel like they've always been a part of me, and I can't imagine the sheer torture it would be to have them cut off.

"Rather ironic, isn't it?" Lilith muses, a sad glint in her ghostly eyes. "While they preach perfection and piety, their actions suggest nothing of the sort."

The table is quiet for a moment as everyone contemplates that awful bit of knowledge. Teddy sighs and stands up.

"Right then, we need to work with you and that spell. Mason and I will key you to our pockets, and you can have a look around and see what you would like to use to eliminate Imogen."

"My vote is a rocket launcher. There's no way she'd survive that." Julian yawns and stretches before reaching for a Danish.

"What happens if she does choose guns? I don't want Glory to get hurt," Ben asks quietly, and Nolan reaches over and squeezes his hand.

"We can make sure she's wearing a vest under her clothes, just to be safe," he reassures Ben, who is gnawing on his lip with worry.

"Also, I can give you this." Lilith waves a hand, and cool, black combat pants and a shirt appear. They look like they are made with some sort of metal, and they shimmer slightly but are completely flexible like cotton.

"What is it?" Ben asks, reaching out to touch the shiny fabric.

"Dragon scales are shaved down then the dust is infused in the material. It is nearly impenetrable," she explains.

"We have dragons in Hell?" Louis sounds like a little kid in a candy store at this information.

"No, not in Hell." Lilith smiles secretly, and Louis's excitement falls.

"So where are they then?" Carter snags a Danish without taking his eye off my grandmother.

"That's a little above your clearance. Maybe one day, I'll share the information."

Luc huffs. "Don't believe her. She's been telling me stories of dragons, unicorns, and mythical creatures for years. I don't believe a word she says."

"You mean creatures like a three-headed dog," Nolan says dryly, and Luc's eyes widen and he gasps. All our gazes drift to Julian, who sits up suddenly and tilts his head to the side like he's listening to something, but then he slumps again.

"Cerberus said it's need to know only, and we don't need to know."

"Asshole," Luc mutters under his breath, pouting.

Shit, time to get back on track and worry about mythical creatures at a far later date.

"How do I kill her? Head shot? Heart shot?" I feel a little sick to my stomach as I ask this, but I know everyone is right, and leaving her alive after this would be stupid.

"Either one works, but they are about the only options. She would survive everything else. If you were good with a sword, I'd recommend decapitation, but that option is out," Leviathan says offhandedly as he devours his plate of food.

"Maybe the rocket launcher is the best choice. Blow her to pieces, there is no coming back from that." Beelzebub points his fork at Julian in agreement and nods.

"I wish I could gift you the power of Hell so just a thought would do it." My grandmother floats around the table slowly, checking out each of my mates and making them squirm in their chairs. If I wasn't so caught up in this very serious conversation, I'd probably be amused.

"It needs to be a brutal, effortless show of power," Luc muses, "to discourage anyone from challenging her again."

"What about a flamethrower?" Mason grins with glee, and my mouth drops open in shock. "Then everyone would be able to watch her writhe and scream in pain. That certainly is a visceral show of power, and the smell of burning flesh will forever remind them of that moment. No one will ever fuck with Glory again."

"Fuck, man, that's barbaric." Louis gags at the thought, but Nolan and Carter exchange a glance.

"You have one of those?" Carter asks Mason.

"Yeah, of course. Don't you?"

"No, actually, we don't." Nolan chuckles, but I'm still horrified that we are calmly discussing how to kill my cousin at breakfast.

"My vote is a crossbow arrow to the heart." Julian opens his eyes from where he's slumped in his chair. "And if we use one with a razor blade tip, we can make sure it's well and truly shredded."

I just stare at him. I have no words.

"Okay, well, it's all well and good to have an argument about weaponry, but unless Glory can do that spell and open one of your chambers in seconds, she's out of luck." Teddy pushes his chair back and leaves me to follow him. I get up and hurry across the large dining hall that's devoid of people, leaving the others to finish their meal in peace and quiet.

"Oh, and when you're all done, you need to come key Glory into your stashes, so we can have a look around. The more options she has, the better," he calls over his shoulder to the rest of my breakfasting family. I just follow behind, trying to shake off the shock. I guess these conversations are going to become an everyday occurrence soon, so I probably have to get used to them quickly or develop a drinking problem.

The guys work with me all day. By the time evening rolls around, and it's time for the challenge, I'm faster but nowhere near as fast as the guys who have been doing it for years. It was a lesson in keeping my face neutral when walking through each individual space. There were some interesting things in each of them, and I didn't want any of my men to feel judged or shamed for their likes or dislikes, but it was Mason's weapons cache that I was most interested in. He had everything from submachine guns and flamethrowers, to flails and even a trebuchet. The guys, as well as Luc and his lieutenants, raved about it, and Mason promised that once the crowning was over and Luc had sorted out his shit with Kerry, they could spend a day launching shit at Mt. Doom. Men! Am I right?

The drive to the colosseum takes about an hour. It's on the opposite side of the city. We take two limos and overtake hundreds, if not thousands, of people all riding Segways to the stadium.

"Fuck me, all these people are coming to see the challenge?" I ask as a group of guys cheers and waves as we pass them.

"Yup, it's a big deal. They all want to see the heir to Hell in action." Julian pats my leg, where my dragon scale combat pants mold perfectly to my body.

"Are they going to be disappointed when I finish it within seconds?" I ask, looking at my uncle for the truth.

He winces, and Luc and Beelzebub grimace, and that gives me my answer. "Yes, probably, but I've arranged for Ed Sheeran to give them a concert afterwards. That should keep them happy."

"Ed Sheeran? He's a demon? Wow, I had no idea."

Luc wiggles on the spot like a little boy caught with his hand in the cookie jar. "No, but he does like to visit Hell. He's a good friend of mine."

"Is he really?" I put Luc on the spot with a glare, thinking maybe this is the kind of situation that Poppy warned me about.

Luc holds up his hand. "I swear. Ed doesn't have to be coerced or mind wiped. He's one of the few humans in the know. He has a holiday home here."

"He's a cool guy. Gets a kick out of the whole Hell thing. Great guy to have beer with," Julian tells me. "He also uses two demon bodyguards, wrath demons, who make his life a lot safer."

"Well, okay then." I stare out the window, biting my lip with nerves. I know we have a plan, and it's solid, but Imogen is the unknown factor. I know nothing about her. They tell me she is arrogant and narcissistic and will want to put on a show, slowly destroying me in front of the demon nation. She won't expect me to finish it there and then. I still haven't settled on what weapon I'm going to use. The guys want me to make it a spectacle, but I'm not sure I can. My human-like sensibilities are already struggling with the fact that I have to kill her. I don't want to make it a spectacle, I just want to put a bullet in her brain and be done with it.

Chapter Thirteen

I sigh heavily as the limousine pulls alongside a replica of the colosseum. There's a red carpet and crowds of people waiting to get a look at who is getting out of the limo. Luc straightens his dress shirt and gives me a wink before climbing out after Leviathan and Beelzebub. The crowd goes wild, and he waves and blows kisses while cameras flash and the two lieutenants stare down anyone who gets too close or handsy with the king.

I slide out of the limo behind my uncle, and the crowd drops into awed silence. The cameras continue to flash, and I paste a serene smile on my face despite feeling incredibly overwhelmed. I wave and step aside for each of my mates to get out of the limo. The crowd's silence doesn't last long as they take in each of my mates. The whispers start up, and before long, there are catcalls and lewd propositions being thrown from all directions. I lose the serene smile and glare.

"Now would be a good time to flex those new

wings of yours," Luc mutters, allowing his to break out from his back. I don't know how it happens, but I can will them to shrink down into my back. Magic, I'm assuming, as the crowd oohs and ahhs at the sight of Luc's. Lilith assured me the magic would allow for any clothes I'm wearing to stay intact, so with a thought, my wings burst free, silencing the noise and intrusive crowd once more.

"Let me make it clear that my mates are off-limits. If I even see someone look at them with lust in their eyes, I will do to you what I'm about to do to Imogen. Let this be your only warning." My voice rings out through the crowd, and I see my face on one of those floating screens across the street from the stadium. I'm scowling, and quite frankly, I wouldn't want to fuck with me. There must be a film crew somewhere, but I can't see them.

"Good job," my uncle mutters under his breath as he holds out a hand and escorts me down the red carpet and into the building. Our mates trail behind us as the crowd watches in silent awe, my warning having kept them quiet.

I heave out the breath I'd been holding when the doors close behind us all. "That was fucking awful." I groan. "Is it always going to be like that?" I ask, retracting my wings, and Luc shakes his head.

"Nope, not always. I'm almost certain that after today, you will go a long way in winning the respect you deserve. It only took me a couple of public beheadings and a few dissidents being thrown into Mt. Doom to quiet the naysayers. You'll be fine."

I gape at him in horror, but Nolan just clamps a hand on my shoulder and gives it a squeeze. "Don't worry, I've got you. I don't mind being your enforcer. In fact, I think I'm going to love it." He releases my shoulder and puts his hands together, cracking his knuckles.

"Oh, I want in on the action," Mason adds. "I have some torture machines that I've always wanted to try out. I want to know exactly how far you can stretch a man before he breaks."

"And Cerberus is dying to turn a few more people into ash for disrespecting you," Julian chimes in, leaning against one of the walls.

"He did that?" Luc's eyebrows jump in surprise, and Julian smirks.

"Yes, your favorite little hostess on the sloth level got a little too big for her boots."

Luc groans. "You killed Sammy?" He sounds disappointed, but Julian shrugs.

"Probably not a bad thing. I am firmly aware that having exes interfere with anything is detrimental to a relationship. Be thankful, because Kerry is never going to have to face her, and I can guarantee Sammy would have made her life hell."

"Good point," Luc agrees as Leviathan and Beelzebub high-five Julian.

"I hated that bitch. She was always putting her hands all over Luc," Leviathan grumbles.

"You slept with her even though you have mates?" I ask him, and he shrugs and points to his chest.

"Lust demon. My mates have given me a free pass until we can bring Kerry to heel. Unfortunately, they haven't been enough to sustain me."

I look at the two men, and for the first time, the arrogance and gruffness they wear like a shield has disappeared, and I see shame.

"We think that Kerry isn't Luc's only mate. We would like to do a search of all earthbound demons because we've exhausted our search here in Hell."

"You've touched every demon in Hell?" I ask, sounding skeptical, and Beelzebub rolls his eyes.

"Yes. Damn man got impatient and held a Cinderella style search. Every eligible demon in the majority was asked to come to the palace and shake hands with Luc. Nada. But there are still a lot of demons on Earth who haven't been tested."

"Well, I will pray that Louis's and Carter's exes are not a match," I tell him dryly, but my mind goes to those I do know who would be good for him. Maybe I'll invite some to tea after my coronation. Our friend Kelly, who planned Bella's wedding, would be a good fit.

"Remind me to give you a membership to my club. A lot of demons go there, that may help,"

Carter tells my uncle, and I screw up my nose. Eww.

"Can we get going please?" I ask, impatient to get this show on the road.

"Yes, of course," Luc agrees as a man finally rushes up to us, shaking his head and wringing his hands.

"Goodness, I am so sorry. The opponent was making some outlandish demands, and I was so caught up in meeting them I missed your arrival," he apologizes, stretching out a hand to my uncle. "Lucifer, so good to see you."

"Ah, Stephen, there you are. I was wondering what the holdup was." Luc shakes the man's hand, and he winces ever so slightly. Despite my uncle's pleasantries, he's obviously annoyed.

"Yes, again, I'm sorry. If you would follow me right this way, I'll show you to your dressing room."

We trail along behind the man who has turned on his heel and is leading us through a maze of corridors that is obviously either under the arena or running alongside the main space.

"How long do we have to wait? I just want to get this over with," I ask, but Luc shushes me. I clench my fists and hiss at him, but Ben grabs my hand, wraps one arm around my waist, and whispers soothing words. I think he wants to avoid any other bloodbaths today, and my uncle really tweaks my temper sometimes.

"Stephen, I don't suppose you happened to hear what Imogen's game plan was going to be," my uncle remarks casually, and the man stops and turns to face him but blanches when he sees him flanked by both of his mates.

"I wish I could tell you, but that would be cheating," he says, looking anywhere but at my uncle.

"Bullshit. Tell me what you know, or you may find yourself cleaning the stands instead of lording over everyone here at the colosseum," my uncle demands, scowling, and Stephen wilts under the fierceness of his stare.

"Fine. She says she's going to toy with her opponent for a little while and show the crowd how unworthy she is to rule before running her through with her sword." He looks at me with fear in his eyes, but all I feel is indifference. We have a plan, and we will execute the plan. Instead of failing, we will succeed.

"Thank you. Now that wasn't so hard, was it?" Luc smirks at the man who just rolls his eyes and stabs a finger at a room.

"This is yours," he says, anger in his voice, before he whirls around and stomps back in the direction we came. "Someone will be back to get you in about half an hour. Be ready."

"What? Damn it, I'm ready now." I follow the others into the room, nervous energy coursing through my body. I just want this over and done with. It's bad enough I'm about to kill someone, but to have to wait to do it is maddening.

"Hey, relax. You've got this." Teddy comes over and squeezes my shoulders while everyone else finds a seat in the lavish waiting room. There's food and drink on a table to one side, and Louis peruses the choices. I'd love to join him, but my stomach is all in knots.

"Okay, let's warm you up." It's Nolan who pushes Teddy away and drags me over to a punching bag hanging on the wall. "She's going to try to get into your head," he says as he walks around to hold it for me.

I make a couple of half-hearted jabs, but I'm too nervous to really put my body into it.

"Glory, snap out of it." Nolan's eyes blaze red as he growls at me. "Come on, channel some of your inner wrath demon. We all know you've got it in you, we've seen the red eyes."

"Ugh, I'm so freaking nervous," I tell him, leaning against the bag instead of punching it. "I don't know how to get worked up."

"Did I tell you why Imogen wants to claim me?" Julian calls from across the room. He's made himself comfortable by stretching out on one of the sofas.

I turn my head but stay where I am, narrowing my eyes. "No, you didn't actually. I just assumed she wants to be Hell's heir and you were the last remaining mate that I wasn't bonded to."

"I mean, yes, there is that, but she could have tried to claim all your mates. In fact, she probably should have. If there's anything that's going to work in making her the next Hell heir, it's claiming all your mates," Julian says, and I start to feel my temper rise. "But it's also because I was super smashed one night and feeling horny, and she offered me a blow job. I took her up on it. She saw the knot and yearned to take a ride on my disco stick, but Levi interrupted us before she could." He waves a hand at the man who grimaces.

"And you thanked me for that when you sobered up."

A growling sound starts to rumble in my chest. "And you're telling me this why? I already explained how hearing about your exes made me feel."

"Did you know that Jenny and Nicole used to come to my club all the time with me and Louis? And for how prissy they look, they are actually both a little freaky. They liked to be spanked and have candle wax dripped all over them while we fucked them from behind and they made out." Carter sits forward in his seat and announces this to the rest of the room.

The rumble in my chest grows louder, and I'm starting to feel a little stabby. Why are these assholes telling me this?

"Oh yeah, I remember that you guys did a performance in the middle of the club once. It was hot as fuck." Mason slides a look in my direction before joining the conversation. "You two were really popular after that. You had no problem feeding your lust, did you?"

"Fuck!" I turn around and smash the bag with my fist. Nolan stumbles slightly before pushing his weight against it. I throw a couple of jabs at it before giving it a side kick. Nolan grunts but holds on.

"Remember that petite little thing in college that you and I tag teamed, Nolan?" Julian calls out. "She had the tightest little pussy, and we wrecked it by double teaming her."

"Agh!" I scream, seeing red and really laying into the bag.

"There it is," I hear Nolan mutter.

In the background, I hear Ben say, "You guys are fucking assholes, you know that?"

Teddy rumbles his agreement.

"Maybe we are, but we got her out of her head and triggered her anger. You don't think Imogen won't do the same sort of thing? Now she can work out the anger and go into the ring clear-headed and thinking straight without any nerves," Mason points out, but I'm still lost in thoughts of my mates with other women.

"Yes, but we also don't want her to tire herself

out," Luc scolds, and I am suddenly frozen, unable to move. "Breathe through the anger, Glory," he whispers to me. Unable to move, all I can do is breathe, so I close my eyes.

"Center yourself. Think about Imogen as a ruler and her subjugating all the citizens of Hell. Think about Nolan's mother and father and your girls. All of them subject to her whims. I can guarantee she will recall all demons from Earth, because she thinks it's a cesspool as well."

My mind flips from my mates with other women to Nolan's parents and my girls. I see them doing hard labor or enslaved to winged beings. Angels! Angels who treat them abysmally. I see Imogen sitting on the throne, smug as shit, while her two cousins crack whips in the direction of the demons of Hell. I can't let that happen.

"Good," Luc whispers. "I can feel your anger still, but now it's focused in the right place. You will win this, because you are doing this for the right reasons. Do not feel guilt. She will be the downfall of Hell if she wins. Without Julian, you can't become the queen of Hell. The power needs to be spread across all of you. I would continue to rule until she can figure out a way to get rid of me, but I wouldn't put it past my brother or father to give her one of their swords to use against me or my mates. As the original demon, it's the only thing that can kill me."

In my mind's eye, I see her standing over my uncle, his wings slashed from his back as she presses the sword slowly through his heart. I can't let any of this happen.

I steel my spine and open my eyes. "I'm ready," I tell him, and he releases me. The first thing I do is flip Julian off.

"You're a fucking asshole," I tell him, and he shrugs.

"It worked though, didn't it? You became a worry wart, Glory, but now you are the warrior you need to be."

"I hate you," I tell him, and he shrugs nonchalantly.

"I'm okay with that if it means you're alive to do it."

I turn my back on him, not looking at my other mates who helped him, and look at my uncle.

"I'm ready."

He nods. "Let it begin."

Chapter Fourteen

The sound of the crowd behind the double doors is thunderous. I stretch my neck to either side and jump up and down on the spot. My focus is narrowed on winning, so I block out everything else, including my mates.

"This is where we leave you. We need to go sit in our box and be seen as not taking sides, although I'm totally rooting for you," Luc tells me before shifting his gaze to my mates. "I think it would be best if you were all seen in my box, looking unconcerned, or at least most of you."

"I will escort Glory into the arena." Nolan crosses his arms stubbornly, and Mason nods.

"Me too, but the rest of you should go. If we crowd Glory, it would look like we are worried about something."

"Of course we're worried," Ben blurts out with tears in his eyes.

"Oh hey, Glory totally has this. It doesn't matter that Imogen has been training all her life for battle, her arrogance will be her downfall," Julian says, patting Ben on the shoulder, but Ben looks unconvinced, and I don't blame him. That wasn't exactly comforting.

"Julian, I think you should shut up now," Louis says, glaring at him.

Julian mimes zipping his lips.

"You know what? Maybe we should just let Imogen have Julian." I turn to my uncle with raised eyebrows. "Do you think she would be happy with that?"

Julian makes a sound of outrage as Luc and his two mates chuckle. "Sure, but I doubt that's going to solve the heir problem. Even if Mom severed your mate potential, I'm pretty sure she would just go after the rest of them as well. She wants the position of heir and will do anything to get it."

"But Lilith said it was her decision."

Lilith appears. "Yes, it is my decision, but truthfully, Imogen has the right bloodline, and she is quite powerful. I mean, there aren't really a lot of other options unless Luc wants to keep doing it," she states matter-of-factly, and I frown. She's changed her tune. I thought she said Imogen would be terrible. Is she using reverse psychology on me?

"Fine, let's just do this," I growl, unwilling to let that woman have anything.

Everyone leaves, Lilith included, and I'm left

with just Mason and Nolan. Through the doors, the crowd's noise dies slightly.

"Ladies and gentlemen, welcome to tonight's mate challenge. The challenge is for Julian Beamus, guardian of the gate," a voice announces, and the crowd roars again.

"Please welcome the challenger to the arena, Lady Imogen Luxure." This time, the crowd's noise isn't as enthusiastic, and there are boos and hisses as music starts to play. The song "We Are the Champions" rings out, drowning out the crowd's annoyance. It seems a little overconfident and presumptuous to me.

I step forward and peer out the door and watch as Imogen enters the arena, wearing a tiny pair of booty shorts and a crop top with a scabbard strapped to her back containing a sword. She's flanked by both of her cousins, and all three of them have faces set like stone.

"You know, I never understood why women dress like that going into battle. Sure, you can move easily, but there's absolutely nothing protecting your skin," I mutter to my guys, and Mason snorts.

"It's for the titillation factor, which might work if she were fighting a guy, but you're not going to be swayed by a bit of skin."

"Hardly," I say dryly as she reaches the middle of the arena and turns in a circle, eyeing the masses with cool detachment.

The arena is very much like what the colosseum in Rome may have looked like in its heyday, with a sand-covered floor and a large, open space with tiered seating stretching skyward. On one side of the arena, I can see a viewing box with Luc seated on a throne, his two mates standing on either side of him. On the throne next to him is Julian, with the rest of my mates seated behind them.

Luc watches on with a blank, imperious stare as Imogen bows mockingly at him. The music cuts out.

"Defending her mate claim is Princess Gloriana Luxure." The crowd falls silent, and "Thunderstruck" by AC/DC starts to play. I smile as I look back at my mates, and Mason is holding a scabbard with a sword in it.

"Wear this, it will throw her off." He helps me slide it onto my back and adjusts it, and the weight of the sword is considerable. "And it's a good backup."

"Will I be able to release my wings with this?" I ask, and he nods.

"Yup, Luc tested it, but remember to leave it until the last minute to shock her. It might make her hesitate, and that's when you nail her."

As much as the guys all tried to convince me to use a flashy weapon, I decided to stick to what I know best, but instead of a nine millimeter, I've chosen something with heavier fire power—a .45

Magnum Desert Eagle. It has a bitch of a recoil, but I'm hoping it's enough to stop her. We also decided that I'd wear it in a holster, and I could reach for it instead of pulling it out of the interdimensional space. As much as I practiced, I still struggled with the words of the damn spell. My hand and mind coordination sucked, and I couldn't do the gestures and say the spell fast enough like the guys, who can practically just think it. The holster is built into the outfit Lilith gifted me.

"A gun?" Lilith reappears and stares in horror as Mason passes me the weapon to put into my holster. "Oh no. No, no, no! You can't fight Imogen with a gun."

I stare at my grandmother in horror. "What the fuck, woman? You were there when we were talking about this."

Lilith shakes her head. "I heard you talking rocket launchers and flamethrowers. Now those would be a spectacle, but a gun? No, no, no. You need to win in a spectacular display so no one will ever doubt you. You'll have to use the sword."

She points to the damn thing strapped to my back.

"Fuck no. I have no clue how to use it," I argue, but a look of determination crosses her face, and she reaches for me with her hands outstretched. I slap them away. "And no, last time you touched me you made me scream," I say, stepping back, but she's quicker than I am, and her hands feel solid on my temples. There's no pain this time, just a bit of warmth before she steps back, looking pleased.

"There, now you have everything you need to beat Imogen." She waves a hand, and the music changes. "Now get out there and beat that bitch. The crowd is restless, and they are going to want to see blood." I listen for a moment and realize I recognize the song and chuckle. It's "Smack my Bitch Up" by The Prodigy, which I guess is really appropriate and probably going to piss Imogen off. I never would have thought Lilith would be a 90's music aficionado.

"But…" I start to argue, and both Nolan and Mason look like they want to as well, but Lilith just holds her hand up.

"Trust me. I want you to rule Hell. I wouldn't do anything to wreck all my carefully laid plans. You have everything you need to win this. Now, are you going to pussy out or be the queen I know you can be?" She raises an eyebrow, and I flip the bitch off. She nods her head, approval shining in her eyes despite the disrespect.

"You've got this, Glory," Nolan tells me, pride and confidence showing on his face, and when I look at Mason, his expression reveals the same thing.

"Let's do this. Hands in, and on three, say, 'Glory, Glory, hell yeah.'" I put my hand out, and my mates follow my lead. Even Lilith's ghostly hand joins the pile.

We do the chant and separate, Lilith disappearing once more with a whispered, "Good luck." Mason and Nolan step out first, and I follow close behind. The crowd falls silent for just a moment before they roar with excitement. Cheers and whistles can be heard over the music as the three of us step forward in sync.

The guys escort me to the middle of the arena where I turn and bow deeply to my uncle with a great sweeping motion. I can hardly contain my surprise that I know how to do that, but obviously Lilith imparted more than how to fight with a sword.

"Gloriana, are you aware this fight is for your mate, Julian Beamus?" Luc asks, his voice booming out around the arena. The crowd falls silent, and anticipation bubbles in the air. "You have the option to concede, but if you don't, then Imogen Luxure will only be triumphant upon your death."

"I do understand, and it will be a cold day in Hell when I give my mate to her," I call, and the crowd roars again.

"Imogen, do you understand that you can concede as well? Otherwise, your death will signal the end of the challenge."

"I understand and have no doubt I will be triumphant over that pathetic creature."

Well, there goes the option of her conceding. I kind of knew she wouldn't, but I still held a small amount of hope that I wouldn't have to kill her.

"Very well. Either of you may concede by laying your weapons down. If that happens, the opponent must immediately stop the fight. Continuing would mean forfeiting. Do you understand?" We both nod, and Luc raises a hand.

"Please leave the arena if you are not participating in the fight." Nolan and Mason both give me a kiss and leave the arena. Imogen's cousins whisper words of encouragement before they, too, hurry out, leaving the two of us alone—or as alone as we can be surrounded by thousands of people.

"When I win, and you die, I will claim those mates too. I will claim them all. I will be a septimax, and Lucifer will have no choice but to declare me Hell's heir. Then, I will spend my days fixing this cesspit and my nights fucking your men."

"Pfft," I scoff. "Lucifer doesn't pick the heir, Hell itself does. I don't know, Imogen… Have you been kind and benevolent to the people around you or a downright bitch?"

For a moment, concern enters Imogen's eyes, but it doesn't last long and is quickly replaced by the familiar arrogance.

"Please, the land will choose me because I am strong and will rule with an iron fist. I will make Hell great, unlike the former ruler."

My eyes slide to my uncle, who is glaring at his niece. Despite the crowd's chants, I know he can hear her.

"Be careful what you say. It's not too late to be smote by said ruler," I sing, but she just grins wickedly.

"He can't do a thing while the challenge is on. I would automatically win."

"Not if you're already dead by his hand," I tell her, and she frowns, thrown off with my declaration.

Luc shouts, "Begin!"

Imogen reaches for her sword—scratch that, swords plural, in her scabbard, pulling both out and twirling them, grinning widely.

"How often did you use swords on Earth?" she taunts as we start to circle one another. With a bend of her knees, she leaps into the air, her wings spread as she dives toward me, swinging both swords.

With a yelp, I duck and roll across the sand, kicking up dirt as she misses me and swoops in the opposite direction.

"Fuck," I exclaim as I scramble to my feet, not letting her get behind me.

She has a manic grin on her face as she stops midair and turns toward me. Narrowing her eyes, she dives straight at me, her swords held out in an attack stance. I scramble to grab my own sword out, but I'm not quick enough and have to leap out of the way again, but not before she slices my arm.

"Fuck." I look down at the large gash across my bicep, blood running freely. Damn, I should have asked for a long-sleeved shirt from Lilith. Growling with annoyance and a small amount of pain, I feel my temper rise. I'm done with this shit.

She laughs with glee as she does a lap around the arena, the crowd throwing obscenities in her direction. She really isn't popular, but she's also distracted, and her arrogance is going to be her downfall.

I get a proper grip on my sword and pull it out, and it's like a chime sounds through the arena. At the same time, I allow my wings to burst free. The crowd falls silent, and you could hear a pin drop. Imogen frowns with confusion before turning back to look at me.

Her grin drops, and she wears a confused frown as she comes to a stop and narrows her eyes on me.

"That's right, bitch. You're not the only one with wings." I kick off the ground and take flight, but her eyes are locked onto the sword in my hand.

I look down at it, and unlike the swords in Imogen's hands, my blade is made of black metal and has a blood-red gem set into the middle of the hilt.

"Is that the Flaming Sword?" Imogen stammers

and turns her glare on my uncle. "Asshole rigged it all along," she mutters.

I look where she is, and sure enough, my uncle has a satisfied grin on his face.

"Oh well, no matter what, I won't be going down without a fight," she shouts and flaps her wings, heading straight for me again. This time, I meet her halfway, and our swords clang together. To my utter amazement, mine cuts right through the one in her left hand. Half the sword drops to the ground, rendered completely useless. My mouth drops open in surprise, which gives Imogen a chance to disengage and put some space between us.

She discards the now useless sword and grips the other one with both hands. "You cheated," she accuses me. "You're using one of the five celestial swords."

Ah, okay, now I see what she's pissed about. It's one of the swords that can supposedly cut through anything, including an angel's wings. Maybe there is an option for me to get out of this without killing her. If I can render her flightless, maybe she will concede. I know it's probably a useless hope, but I really don't want to kill my cousin. I can't imagine that's going to go well for family relations.

Imogen makes another dive at me, and I use my own wings to bat her out of the way. As she falls through the air, I swipe out with my sword, and sure enough, it cuts through her wing like butter. Her scream is filled with agony as her right wing flutters to the ground, leaving behind a bloody stump. The crowd gasps with shock as Imogen loses control and careens sideways, hitting the ground with a thud.

I drop to the ground, closing my wings tightly against my back, and walk over to her as she sobs, her blood staining the sand behind her.

Before I can lose my nerve, I swipe out with my sword again and sever her other wing from her back, leaving behind two, clean-cut bloody stumps. Nausea rolls through me, and I feel like gagging, but I hold my ground. Her scream of agony pierces my soul, but I have to remember she was willing to kill me.

"Concede now, and I will let you live," I tell her quietly so no one can hear me.

She looks up at me with a tear-streaked face, some of the dust from the ground smudged across one of her cheeks, but her eyes glitter with malice.

"You only won because Luc rigged this fight. If you didn't have that sword, I would have been triumphant."

I shrug. "Maybe, but we will never know. Now, do you concede? Lay your weapon on the ground, and I will allow you to live as long as you stay away from my family. Maybe I'll banish you to Earth to live out your days, stripped of any power you have," I say, not taking my eyes off her. Her wings are gone, and she is in complete agony, but she still has two legs and two arms, and she hasn't agreed to anything yet.

I see her mulling over my words. It's a fair offer. Her only other option is death, so surely she would prefer to live.

She drops her head and nods once. "I concede." She releases her weapon, and the arena bursts into screams and applause.

I look toward my uncle, who has gotten to his feet, waiting for him to declare me the winner. He's smiling, and he opens his mouth to speak, but that smile drops, and he lifts a hand and shouts, "Look out!"

Stupid me, I should have kicked the sword away from her reach. She lunges for it and lashes out. I feel it slash across my calf, but my pants protect me. Imogen doesn't make it to her feet before my sword passes through her neck, severing her head from her shoulders.

I watch on with cold detachment as her head tumbles from her neck and rolls across the sandy ground, her eyes and mouth wide with shock. Her body crumples to the ground, joining her wings, while the rest of her life blood spills out, turning the sand a rosy pink.

Chapter Fifteen

The crowd is silent, and dread fills my soul over my actions, but before I can do anything else, something leaps out of the stands. I hold my sword up, expecting it to be one of Imogen's cousins coming at me for revenge, but it's not. It's a three-headed dog. He lands at my feet, lifts a leg, and pisses on Imogen's corpse before turning around and breathing onto her wings, followed by her body. They go up in flames, and the crowd goes mad once more as Imogen's remains quickly turn to ash.

"Glory, Glory, Glory," they chant as Cerberus approaches me and nudges my hand with one of his heads. I roll my eyes and give him a scratch behind the ears on each head.

"Ladies and gentlemen, the undeniable winner of the mate challenge is Gloriana Luxure, and also your heir."

Demons cheer and clap and throw flowers onto the sand, and staff members run through doors surrounding the arena. Some pick up the flowers and bring them to me, some sweep away the evidence that Imogen ever existed, and even more bring out trucks with trailers of sound and stage equipment.

I mutely take the flowers, nodding my thanks before half-heartedly waving to the crowd. I have mixed feelings—incredible guilt because I killed her, and immense relief because I won't always be looking over my shoulder.

"To celebrate Glory's victory, I have a surprise for you. One of Hell's favorite performers has agreed to entertain you this evening. Joining us once the arena has been cleansed and outfitted is my good friend, Ed Sheeran."

I thought the crowd had been ecstatic when I won, but the noise is now indescribable. I'm still kind of floundering when Cerberus nudges me, and I stumble before moving in the direction he's herding me in.

In a daze, I limp back the way I came, the crowd having forgotten about me in their impending joy over Ed. Although she didn't cut through my combat pants, I'm pretty sure I'll have a bruise where she tried to slice me with her sword. When I get back to the staging area, Nolan and Mason are waiting for us.

Both of them hug me, and with Cerberus's help,

they direct me to a first aid staffer who takes a look at the cut on my arm.

"Babe, you were amazing," Mason gushes as Nolan stands there with his arms crossed, glaring at the person looking over my arm.

The medic swallows nervously, and I don't blame him. It must be nerve-racking having the wrath demon stare at him like that.

"You're going to need a couple of stitches, just until your natural healing kicks in. We should be able to remove them in a couple of days," he says, looking between me and Nolan.

"Just ignore him and do what you have to. You didn't do this to me," I tell him but glare at Nolan.

Cerberus flops down at my feet but keeps all six eyes on the medic. The poor bastard is starting to sweat now.

It takes more than a few stitches, it's at least twelve, but he numbed it up and then slaps a water-proof bandage on it when he's done, giving me instructions about keeping it dry and not taxing myself, before leaving the four of us alone again.

"How are you really?" Nolan squats down in front of me once the medic has gone, concern in his eyes. "That couldn't have been easy, but she didn't give you a choice."

"She was never going to surrender," Mason says, agreeing with Nolan, and I sigh with sadness.

Cerberus licks my hand, and I reach down to

scratch the head that licked me. I giggle when the other two want in on the action, pleased to have something else to think about for a moment.

"No, I know, but I couldn't have lived with myself if I didn't at least give her a choice. Did you guys know that was Luc's own personal sword?" I ask them, and both shake their heads.

"No, he was the one who approached us and said it would look better if you at least wore it into the fight," Mason explains.

"And Lilith then insisted I needed to use it. I don't know, but I think maybe Imogen was right and they both cheated."

Nolan nods. "Maybe they did, but don't forget that she was the one who started it. She didn't have to challenge you, and to be honest, if she had the choice, she wouldn't have played by the rules either."

Mason and Nolan exchange a look. "We weren't going to tell you this, but she was watching you last night, and she tried to follow you to the club. Luc's guards put a stop to it, but what do you think would have happened if she did get a chance to get to you early?"

"She would have killed me," I answer dully.

Cerberus stands up and stretches, his butt wiggling in the downward dog pose, bringing a smile to my face. Each head then gives me a lick on the hand before his body shimmers and Julian appears naked before us.

"What's done is done. Good riddance to bad rubbish, I say," he tells me and holds out a hand.

"Now, if you boys will excuse us, Glory and I have a prior engagement."

I glare at his hand, still pissed that he once again threw his conquests in my face despite it being for a good cause.

"You're an asshole," I say, slapping his hand away, and he frowns.

"Yeah, I am, I won't deny it, but I won't apologize for doing what I had to do. Glory, the reason you're going to be a good ruler is because you are kind and compassionate, but sometimes you need a bit of ruthlessness as well, and I guess that's the reason I'm one of your mates. I won't shy away from the dirty jobs. I may be lazy, but that's what makes me effective. I want the job done as efficiently and as quickly as possible. Take me as I am, I'm never going to change or ask your grandma to sever our bond."

He has a stubborn set to his jaw now, and he crosses his arms, staring me down. A few staff members hurry by the medical room, but they must stop and turn around, because when they pass back in the opposite direction, they are slow and stare at my naked mate with hunger in their eyes.

I jump to my feet and take a step in their direction, annoyed they would even dare to look at him. Despite being pissed at Julian, he is still mine.

"New rule. No shifting in public where everybody can see you naked," I snarl at the annoying shifter who just smirks.

"You know what? We're just going to go let the rest of the guys know you're okay and tell Luc he doesn't need to teleport you anywhere." Mason chuckles and gives me a kiss. "Give him hell, baby," he whispers before backing away.

Nolan still wears a frown, but there is amusement in his eyes. "I might just return this to Luc." He picks up the sword from where I discarded it, grimacing at the blood and gore stuck to the blade. "Maybe he can use magic to clean it." He helps me shrug out of the scabbard carefully so I don't hit the newly stitched wound on my arm before he, too, gives me a kiss. "Give him hell. He is all bluster, but he does like it when you pull his hair and praise him while you fuck," he whispers in my ear, and my eyes widen slightly. Huh, Julian said he loved riling Nolan up, but who would have guessed he liked to be dominated and had a praise kink? I kind of thought the two of them wrestled violently for dominance.

Mason and Nolan leave, pulling the door closed behind them, leaving Julian and I alone. I feel awkward as fuck as I look around the medical bay. There is a bathroom off to one side. I look down at myself and notice I'm covered in dirt, grime, and blood splatter from Imogen, not to mention my own blood.

"Want to shower with me?" I ask my unbonded mate, nodding at the bathroom.

A grin crosses his lips, and he nods. "Sounds fun. I'll wash your back if you'll wash mine." He winks flirtatiously at me, but I can see some uncertainty in his eyes.

"You're an asshole, you know," I tell him, putting my hands on my hips.

He sighs and sidles up next to me, putting his hands over mine and giving me a gentle kiss on the lips. "I know, but I didn't know what else to do to get you out of your head. Forgive me?"

"Sure, because it worked, but never again. Seriously. Find something else to make me mad. Tell me you ate the last of my favorite cupcakes, or Cerberus chewed on my favorite pair of shoes. Anything but throwing your exes in my face. I am not ashamed to admit I'm still a little insecure. Give me a few months to settle into this eight-way relationship and feel secure in my place in it."

"Ah, babe, you are the very center of it. The sun that we all revolve around. Your beauty and kindness is so blinding, none of us have any intention of looking anywhere else."

I feel a blush spread across my cheeks at his words. "Come on, I want to get clean." I grab his hand and tow him to the bathroom. I'm weirdly nervous. Everything happened naturally with the rest of them, and I really don't know where to start.

I strip, and Julian's eyes remain locked on my naked body as I turn on the water. When it hits the right temp, I step in, groaning as I stick my head under the steaming hot water and allow it to flow over me. I push my hair back out of my face before opening my eyes, then I turn so my wings get cleaned as well. Hopefully that's how you do it. I'm just praying that they don't end up waterlogged and drag me down, but it seems like they are hydrostatic. I give them a little shake, and the water flies off them. I smirk as I take in my mate. His eyes are hooded with desire, and his hand strokes his thick cock, which seems very happy to see me.

"Well, are you getting in or not?" I ask, and he steps into the shower, his eyes holding mine. He pushes me up against the wall, releasing his cock to push against my stomach as he leans down and takes my mouth with his. His lips are soft and pillowy as his tongue slides along the seam of my mouth, asking for entrance. I don't hesitate to let him in as I wrap my arms around his body and pull him tightly against me, remembering Nolan's words.

Steam drifts around us as the water flows over Julian's body, wetting his hair so it hangs in messy strands around his face. His hands slide over my skin as our wet bodies move together, my breasts pressed against his hard lines. As his hands drift over my curves, exploring every inch, I'm surprised to feel calluses scratching against my skin. I expected his hands to be soft and supple, but it seems I may have underestimated my sloth mate.

I nibble gently on his lip before nipping a little harder. His gasp and the outbreak of gooseflesh across his arms make me smile. I softly stroke his long hair, pushing it back from his face before grabbing it and pulling his mouth away from mine.

"How about you be a good boy and get on your knees and show your queen how badly you want to be her mate?" I watch as his pupils contract with pleasure and his breathing hitches.

His tongue darts out, and he licks a drop of water off his lip before I release his hair and push his shoulder. He kneels at my feet, and I look down and smirk. Seeing him look up at me with dazed, lust-filled eyes is a heady feeling.

"Good boy," I purr, stroking his cheek, and his whole body shudders. I pull my wings in tight against my back and lean backward. I can feel how cold the tiles are through my wings and grimace. I reach up and adjust the spray so it's now pointing at the wall, warming me and the tiles, and nod to Julian to adjust. He shuffles forward, paying no attention to the tiles biting into his knees. I lift a foot and hook it over his shoulder, using it to draw him closer to my body and give him better access to my pussy.

He dives in and licks a line from my entrance to my clit, and I shudder with the sensation. My knees grow weak, so I grab onto his head for purchase. His tongue is bigger, wider, and longer than a human tongue. "Holy fuck."

I look down at him, and he smirks up at me before diving back in. My eyes just about roll back in my head from the sensations as I entwine my hand in his long, white locks and tug. "You look so pretty at my feet with your face in my cunt," I tell him, and I feel him groan against me.

He reaches down with one hand and palms his shaft, roughly tugging on it a couple of times. He stabs his tongue in and out of my tight channel, and I feel my walls flutter as he gets deeper than any man before him. Holy fuck. My head drops back against the wall, and I close my eyes, as my body tightens with exquisite tension.

"Enough," I say and gently tug him to his feet by his hair. His eyes are wide and glassy as he licks his lips, that long tongue flicking out to grab every last drop of my desire.

"Are you ready to become my mate?" I ask him when we're face to face.

"Honey, I've been ready since the moment I laid eyes on you," he replies and leans in to kiss me. This one isn't as sensual as the last. This kiss is full of fire and passion as one of his hands drifts up to my breast and caresses it, his other slipping down to my ass to pull me against his hard length. We both groan into each other's mouths when he grinds against me, my eyes widening at the feeling of the bump at the base.

His hands leave my body, and he reaches up and strokes my wings.

"Oh my god." I heave out a gasp of air. It's like he has a direct connection from my wings to my clit.

He winks. "Levi did me a solid and told me how sensitive they are to mates. Now turn around for me."

He gently spins me and pushes me forward. "Hands against the wall, princess," he tells me. I brace myself as he continues to run his hands over my feathers, and my whole body shudders. My nipples tighten even more than I thought they could, and my core throbs painfully.

I feel him notch himself at my entrance. Slowly and tortuously, he presses inside, and I moan as my head hangs, my hair creating a barrier in front of me.

"This is going to be fast, sweetheart. I'm barely hanging on as it is," he whispers in my ear, brushing his chest against my wings, and I shudder from the riot of sensations it creates.

"Do it," I demand, and his hands glide to my

hips as he withdraws inch by inch. I sob when he slides slowly over my G-spot. "God, that feels so good. You're so big and perfect for me," I mutter, remembering how he likes to be praised, but I'm almost past the point of coherency. My nerves are aflame with passion, and my mind is fogged with the need for release.

"Stop torturing me," I demand gutturally. "Be a good boy and fuck your queen."

His hands tighten on my hips, and his fingers dig in hard enough to leave bruises as he lunges forward. I push back to meet his thrusts. His pace becomes punishing, our breaths heaving as one, the only sound apart from the gentle rush of water. Every stroke is hard as the knot at the base of his cock tries to breach my pulsing entrance. With one last fierce thrust, I shout his name as it finally pushes past my resistance and starts to swell. My core convulses, and a searing bolt of pleasure flows through my veins as his knot swells even bigger, vibrating ever so slightly. My fingers try to grab onto something, but the tiles make it impossible. His head drops to my back as he shudders, a deep groan echoing throughout the quiet room as he fills my pussy with his cum.

My body trembles repeatedly as pleasure rolls over it like an out of control freight train. I taste blood as I bite down on my lip to control my screams of enjoyment. Slowly, his hands leave my hips and slide upwards until they find purchase on my breasts. He nuzzles my wings out of the way and nips my neck, his knot pulsing again and causing another sharp ripple of pleasure to skim across my nerve endings. A smug and triumphant feeling echoes around inside my chest as our mate bond solidifies.

"Wow," I murmur, and that smugness grows, practically preening inside my chest. I want to scoff, but he kind of deserves all the praise.

"Told you I'd rock your world," he mutters, leaning in to kiss me before nuzzling his cheek against mine. He helps me stand more upright, crowding in close. "We're going to be stuck here a little while. Let me wash you," he says, reaching over my shoulder to pump some shampoo into his palm. He then proceeds to gently wash my hair. The head massage he gives me, combined with the occasional pulse of his cock, is enough to convince me I died at Imogen's hand and went to Heaven.

"Fine, maybe I'll keep you," I mutter, blissed out beyond belief.

Chapter Sixteen

Once his knot deflates and we can separate, Julian and I finish up in the shower, washing ourselves leisurely and taking a quiet moment just for us. I know things are about to blow up, and I need a minute to breathe.

When we turn off the water and dry ourselves, we find a pile of clothes for each of us waiting on a table in the locker room. One of the guys must have snuck in and left them for us. Once Julian pulls on his sweats, socks, and shoes, he leans back against the lockers and watches as I do the same thing. "How are you feeling?" he asks carefully, and when I look up, there is a hint of concern in his eyes.

I smile, trying to ease his worry. "I feel fucking amazing actually. It's like I'm finally whole, and this weight inside my chest that I hadn't even noticed I was carrying has lifted."

The concern is still in his eyes, so when I finish tying my laces, I sidle up to him and wrap my arms around his waist, leaning my head against his chest. "I love you," I tell him, and I hear him gasp. "Even if you are a giant A-hole who I'm sure is going to cause lots of drama in our family." I look up at him and smirk, but there are unshed tears in his eyes. "Oh shit, hey, what's wrong?"

He shakes his head and presses a kiss to my forehead. "Nothing's wrong, I'm just incredibly fucking happy. I always felt like I was missing something. I thought it was Nolan, but it turns out it was all of you. My chest feels the same as yours, full of love and happiness."

"Well, this is all sweet and everything, but we need to get going." Both of us startle and turn our heads to find my uncle standing in the doorway to the locker room looking peeved. "Can you two hurry it up? I want to do this thing and get back in time to see the second half of Ed's show."

I'm assuming he means my official crowning as Hell's ruler as opposed to the fake for show one at the end of the week.

"Nice to see you have your priorities straight," I tell my uncle, pulling away from my new mate, but all he does is turn me around to face Lucifer then pull me back against his chest, wrapping his arms around my waist. It looks like he's feeling as needy for touch as I am. "I would have thought you'd head to Earth and chase Kerry down." I reach back and pull my wet hair over my shoulder so it's not soaking into Julian's chest. Using the hair tie from my wrist, I quickly braid it and tie it off.

"Harrumph, no. I'm not allowed to leave Hell until after the fake crowning. I'm not even opening the portals until just before."

"But you are going to let my family in, aren't you?" I ask, and he nods.

"Yes, I will open it a few hours before the scheduled crowning and escort them back myself." He grins. "I can't wait to see Petra's face when she sees me. She's going to die." He rubs his hands together with glee, and I snort.

"No, dude, you're going to wish you had when she finds out I'm now ruling Hell." I point at him, and his grin drops, and I can see his skin visibly pale.

"Holy fuck, you're right. Maybe I'll send Levi and Beezle instead," he mutters, approaching us.

"Pussy." Julian laughs, and Luc shakes his head.

"Nah, man, you wait and see. My sister is a force to be reckoned with. Just make sure you keep her girl happy, or you will be on the receiving end."

Luc puts a hand on each of us, and within seconds, we are back under Mt. Doom in the stifling hot cave. My grandmother's incorporeal form is here, and she is much brighter in the center of her power than she was when she came to the palace. Now, she looks almost solid again.

"Glory!" Ben shouts, and before I can blink, he

has both arms wrapped around Julian and me, hugging us tightly. "Thank goodness you are okay. I was so worried when she got that first hit in." Ben pulls away, and Carter and Louis crowd into me, sandwiching me between them. Julian grunts as he gets caught between them too.

"You were amazing," Carter tells me, kissing me lightly as Louis winds his arm around Julian's and my waists, pulling us against him.

"You were *très magnifique*, my little sugar plum. I'm still hard from watching you." My eyebrows jump as Julian grumbles about a dick in his ass and being overcrowded, but I can tell from the feelings inside my chest that he is happy to be in this position.

That's right, when the last bond snapped into place, my chest didn't just fill with love. I can now pick up faint feelings from all of my mates. Just now, Ben was stressed and nervous, but trying to be brave. Both Louis and Carter also have a hint of worry, but pride overshadows it.

I can feel Teddy's impatience, and he finally reaches his limit and grabs me out of Julian's arms, pulling me from between Louis and Carter. I chuckle as Julian ends up squished between them instead. Both Louis and Carter smirk as Carter leans in and whispers something in Julian's ear. I can't hear what he says, but Julian's feelings inside my chest change from contentedness to intrigued and a little bit horny.

"Glory." My name on Teddy's lips is like a benediction. "That must have been so hard for you." He wraps me in his solid arms, and my body shudders. Teddy's feelings are warm, gentle reassurance and understanding. Mason joins our snuggle and presses a kiss to my head, and for a moment, we just exist. Everything that is about to happen is a mere shadow none of us want to think about.

"Yes, yes." Lilith circles us as we break apart, her eyes narrowed and lips pursed. "This is just as I expected. Your bond is solid and strong, so this might just work."

"Hold up. Are you saying it might not?" I ask her, and she shrugs her delicate shoulders.

"I am a god, Glory, and my power is being passed to you mere mortals. Even my own son, who is full god, could not contain my full power. You are only half god. Thankfully, each and every one of your men have the original bloodline flowing through their veins. Each and every one of the original angels had a little bit extra in their makeup gifted to them from me and my husband. This has to work," she says almost desperately, and Nolan glares at her.

"Is this going to harm Glory?" It's so sweet that he's not even thinking of himself.

"Or any of them?" I add. "Nolan has two little girls at home who won't recover if anything happens to us."

"It will either work or it won't. None of you should be harmed, maybe singed a little with a power overload that will take a few days to recover from, but you will be alive and fully functioning no matter the outcome." Sometimes my grandmother has the callousness of a being who has lived too long and seen too much. "Shall we get started?" She waves her hand with a flourish, and a flame appears in the middle of the room. Heat radiates off it as it flickers red, orange, and blue, but as we step a little closer, urged by Lilith, I see something floating within the flame.

"Glory, if you and your mates could please form a circle around the flame and hold hands…" Lilith directs us before waving my uncle over. "Luc, please join them. You two will get injured if you stay. Go back to the palace and wait. Luc will be fine." She dismisses Luc's mates with a wave of her hand, and the two giant men disappear. "Right, Luc, stand next to Glory."

Luc looks annoyed that she dismissed his mates just like that, but he holds his tongue and takes my hand. I'm not paying any attention, though, because I'm trying to see what is floating in the flames.

"Is that..." I trail off, because I'm not exactly sure what I'm looking at.

"That's the crown of Hell. Whoever wears it and carries my sword, the sword of creation, is the ruler, but they needed to be cleansed before I could pass them on to you." I watch in amazement as she reaches in and pulls out the flaming, red-hot crown. It's made of the same black metal as Lucifer's sword, with many blood-red gems set into each of the spikes sticking up from the band. She turns and steps toward me, holding the crown, which is still flaming, out in front of herself. I guess being incorporeal helps in these kinds of situations—no third degree burns.

"Gloriana, I bestow upon you the authority and power to rule Hell and the citizens that reside within it. Make wise choices and defend this land with your heart and soul. When I place this crown upon your head, do not let go of each other's hands. Luc's ruling power needs to drain into you."

"Will that leave him powerless?" I ask, concerned for my uncle, and Lilith laughs out loud, a tinkling sound despite the seriousness of the situation.

"Heavens no. The bastard will still have way too much power. He is my son, after all."

Luc squeezes my hand in gratitude or reassurance. I'm not sure why, but it is comforting.

"Wait, isn't that going to burn her?" Ben asks, and his worry aches inside my chest.

"Yes, I'm afraid it will, but there is no reward without suffering," Lilith announces before placing the crown on my head, not waiting for me to back out.

The excruciating pain is instant, and I try to pull my hands free so I can grab it and tear it off, but it's like we are all locked together. I scream louder than I've ever screamed before, and tears flow down my face from the sheer agony, but the pain on my head soon pales in comparison to the onslaught that rips through my body.

What can only be described as pure, raw, undiluted power rips through me like a freight train, turning me to ash and rebuilding me from the ground up. Then, it radiates down my arms to Nolan, spreading out around the circle to each of my mates before ending with Julian who is linked on the other side of Luc.

I watch through tears of horror as each of them also experience the same kind of pain as I do. The cavern echoes with screams of agony. Luc and Lilith are silent, but Luc grits his teeth. Slowly and surely, the power starts to die down, but I watch each of my mates succumb to the pain and pass out, falling to the ground one by one. We drop hands, and Lilith conjures mattresses to catch them as they fall, until only Luc, Lilith, and I are still standing.

The pain and flames disperse, and I feel myself wobble as it all settles into my body. Luc quickly steadies me.

"Are they okay?" I rasp, my throat aching from screaming, unable to take my eyes off my unconscious mates.

"Yes, they will be fine. It worked, and now they need to sleep off the overload of power while Luc and I show you exactly what you are capable of." Lilith sounds smug and pleased, and I kind of want to smack her, but despite how good that would feel, that would be disrespectful.

I roll my shoulders and steel my spine, pushing away Luc's hands so I can stand on my own. Despite feeling like I could sleep for a hundred days and the worry I feel for my mates, I want to take the crash course to Hell so I can get on with the rest of our lives. I'm ready to do what I need to do.

I blow out a huge breath, and when I look at my grandmother, she gasps in shock. "Your eyes!" she comments, and my uncle steps in front of me and reaches out to hold my chin so he can get a better look. A pleased grin crosses his lips.

"Looks like this worked better than you hoped, Mother," he says, dropping his hand and conjuring a mirror. He holds it up so I can see it. Gone are the light blue pupils, and in their place are irises that look like galaxies. They swirl and shift and are quite intimidating.

"Oh my god." I reach up and press a hand to my cheek as I stare into the mirror. Sure enough, that's my face and hand.

"I had eyes like that before I gave all my power to form Hell. My ex-husband still has eyes like that. I would guess he's going to be a little thrown off at your first meeting. I wish I could stick around for that," Lilith explains, sounding pleased.

Her words register, and Luc gets rid of the mirror as I face my grandmother. I want to ask her what she means by that, but I can already tell. She's fading, almost nothing is left of her now.

"Teach her everything she needs to know, my boy," she says faintly, reaching out to cup his face.

"I love you, both of you, and I will return." That's the last thing she says before she winks out of existence. I hear my uncle whimper slightly, and I wrap an arm around his waist as the two of us take a moment to grieve.

"She will be back," I reassure him, and he sighs heavily before pulling away.

"Of course she will, but how long that will take, I have no idea."

"Well, it's not like we don't have the time to wait… or do we? Are you mortal now?"

"Nobody knows for sure. I would guess because our parents are immortal that I will be too. Both your mother and I are very old. Whether our mates will also become immortal or we become mortal like our mates is anyone's guess. Okay, my powerful little niece…" The sadness clears and is replaced with excitement. "Are you ready to rumble?"

Chapter Seventeen

After giving me brief instructions to sleep, Luc returned to the Ed Sheeran concert. I made sure that every one of my mates was still breathing before curling up next to Nolan and taking a much needed nap. I'm not sure how long I slept for, but before I knew it, Luc returned and shook my shoulder.

"Come on, let's get to it."

He spent the next four days teaching me everything I needed to know about the power coursing through my veins. The crown itself was an interesting lesson. Luc told me that it will always magically appear when I am in public. It's corporeal in that I can take it off and on, but it's magical in that it appears and disappears at whim.

Lilith's sword of creation is also mine as well, but it is locked away in a safe that only I can access, which is magically attuned to my power and my power only. It won't open if it registers anyone else in the vicinity. It's too powerful and destructive toward myself, my mates, and my family members to leave it lying about.

Luc tells me that once every three months, I will need to meet with God for any angels who have been deemed unworthy. Thankfully, God is responsible for cutting their wings off so I don't even really need the sword, but it makes a good impression and reminds God that he's not the only one with power. Luc says he will continue to attend the meetings with God with me mostly because he thrives on pissing off his father.

The power of Hell is mind-boggling, and it's a lot to take in, but the day of the "official" crowning has finally arrived, and I think I have a handle on it. I'm not even worried that I am going to be coming face-to-face with the evil that is Mabuz soon. The power coursing through me has the potential to make me unfeeling, but when my mates finally woke up from their extended slumber, it balanced out with their affection and understanding.

Mabuz is still an insignificant slug, though, and I will take great pleasure in making sure he's never going to hurt another person at all.

"Lucifer Morningstar Luxure!" My mom's shrill voice has us all wincing in the waiting room off to the side of the throne room. The ceremony is being held here and broadcast to all of Hell. There are parties being thrown all over the city in honor of this occasion, which is all being paid for by the crown.

She strides into the room, looking like perfection in her gorgeous, long-sleeved black ball gown with threads of red and pale pink running through the skirt.

We've been waiting here for all the guests to arrive. My men are all wearing matching dark maroon suits with black shirts. Their suits match my dress perfectly, which is velvet and off the shoulder and full, like Cinderella. I really feel like a queen in it. The matching gems that go with the crown don't hurt either. Beautiful, blood-red ruby drop earrings and an elaborate filigree necklace with inlaid red rubies and black diamonds glisten in the light.

"Petra!" he exclaims and holds his arms out with a big smile, but that quickly falls when she slaps him across the face.

"How dare you choose my daughter as your replacement." Her eyes are narrowed, and her lips are pursed. I consider moving out of the firing line, but I really do owe my uncle everything.

He rubs his cheek and goes to say something, but I step between them.

"Mom, you look beautiful." I try to distract her, and it works slightly. Her scowl softens as she takes me in, but tears well in her eyes.

"I didn't want this for you, baby," she tells me, hugging me tightly.

"Don't blame Luc. It was Hell itself that chose me," I explain, not mentioning Lilith because she asked us not to.

She pulls away and blanches when she sees my eyes. "You have eyes like my mother," she sobs quietly.

"Oh, Mom, don't worry, I'm not upset. I'm looking forward to it actually."

"But you won't be able to leave," she argues, and I smile smugly.

"Actually, that's one of the things that's changed with my rule. Luc wasn't allowed to leave because he contained most of the power of Hell, but as long as all eight of us don't leave at the same time, we can come and go as we wish."

Mom's sigh of relief is huge. "Good, because I really didn't want to have to tell everyone we were moving back to Hell."

"I'll put a private portal in a spare room at your house. You won't even have to leave to come visit," I assure her as my dads lose patience and push her out of the way. All three of them give me kisses and hugs and congratulate me. All around the room, my family is chatting with my mates and being introduced to Julian. My brothers look handsome in their charcoal suits.

"Well, bitch, who would have thought, queen of the world?" My dads step out of the way, revealing Serena in a gorgeous, sleek, mermaid style gown with her blond hair piled elegantly on top of her head.

"Not me," I reply as I wrap my arms around her and hug her. "I've missed you," I whisper, and she nods as she steps back.

"I've missed you too. When this little shindig is over, I want all the tea." She looks at Julian and winks. "Mate challenge and all."

"I killed our cousin," I say flatly, and she shrugs as Mom joins us.

"That bitch deserved it. We watched the video of it when we got here. You were amazing, and you have fucking wings," Serena says with obvious jealousy, eyeing them behind me like she wants to run her hands over them.

"So does Mom." I point to her, throwing her under the bus as well, trying to distract my sister. I've discovered it's kind of an intimate thing to touch one's wings, or that's what it's like when my mates touch them.

Serena's eyes widen, and she turns to our mother. "You do?"

Mom sighs and shakes her shoulders. Out pops the most gorgeous white wings with baby pink tips. She shudders, and so do the wings as she stretches her neck from side to side.

"Ugh, that feels good. It's been a while."

"Whoa." Seth and Silas join our circle, their

eyes wide with shock as they take in Mom's wings. It's not long before Callen and Kade do as well.

"No fair. Why don't we have wings too?" Kade asks.

"You do." Luc joins us and looks at me, raising an eyebrow. I blanch, remembering the pain that Lilith caused me when she yanked them out.

"It's going to hurt," I warn them, but all five of my siblings demand that I give them their wings.

Half an hour later, all five of them are groaning and cursing at me, but I do the right thing and impart the innate knowledge of how to use their wings, so they don't struggle to learn to fly. I'm benevolent like that.

"Now, remember, wings are for Hell only. No showing them off when you're on Earth. What Glory giveth, Glory can taketh away." As one, all five of them flip me off.

"Mom!" two little voices shout over all the rest of the noise, and I look to the doorway. Standing there are my babies. I don't wait, I pick up my skirt and hurry toward them, knocking Julian and Ben out of the way in my haste to get to them. I drop down onto my knees and hold out my arms, but they skid to a stop, their eyes wide as they take in my wings.

"You're an angel," Aria whispers with amazement.

I shake my head. "No, sweetie, I'm still a demon." I don't ever want her to confuse the two.

"I want wings too, Mommy." Zoe moves around so she can reach them and runs her hand through them. I brace for how that's going to feel, but it doesn't feel anything like my mates' touch, thankfully.

"Oh, my angel children, I'm sorry, but wings are for people in my family only," I explain, and both of their bottom lips drop.

"But aren't we in your family?" Aria crosses her arms stubbornly, and my heart aches.

"Of course you are." A voice behind me has me turning to look up at my uncle. He's beaming at the girls as he kneels down with us. "Hi, I'm Uncle Luc. I'm pretty sure if Glory says the magic words, then she can give you wings as well."

The girls smile shyly at him. "You're pretty," Zoe tells him, and he preens as I roll my eyes.

My mind goes back to our days of training, and Luc telling me I can literally do anything I put my mind to with the right amount of intent.

"Is it going to hurt them like it did the others?" I ask, nodding to my siblings who are still moaning as they play with their wings, jumping into the air and flapping a little before settling down. The grins on all their faces are enough to make my day.

"Shouldn't. With theirs, you were pulling them out from where they were trapped. You're gifting them to the girls. While you're at it, maybe give them to your mates, mine, and your mother's as well. Then, we can go on family flying trips to explore Hell." He sounds giddy with the idea, and I can't help but grin at him. My uncle is such a sap. "Not to mention what a stir it will cause when we go out there for the ceremony."

My grin falls as I think about all the angels out there who have had their wings cut off, not to mention the rest of the Hell residents who never got the opportunity to have them, and a sense of determination washes over me. I know Luc used the power of Hell for silly things, but I'm going to start my rule the right way.

Closing my eyes, I think about everyone residing in Hell having wings, and the knowledge to use them, then I will it to be.

A burst of power flows out of me, and shouts of surprise cause me to open my eyes and look around the room. Everyone who didn't have wings before are now sporting a fantastic set. The sound of wings rustling is deafening as everyone gapes at their new appendages in amazement. Unlike angel wings, which are predominantly white, the wings in this room are a rainbow of colors. Ben's are actually rainbow colored, and he is clapping his hands with excitement.

"No bitch will out drag me now!" he crows with glee.

I look down at the girls and their delicate little feathered wings behind them. Both of theirs sparkle with glitter and couldn't be more appropriate for them.

"Wow." Nolan's mom and dad, who entered with the girls, are looking at their own wings with amazement. "Thank you, Glory," Evelyn says with tears in her eyes.

Shouts from the throne room draw our attention, and Luc pokes his head out. When he comes back, his mouth is open with shock.

"What did you do?" he exclaims, and I shrug.

"Gave everyone what they should have had from the start," I tell him, not wanting to make a fuss. "Shall we get this show on the road now that everyone is here?"

I wave my hand and put an individual protective barrier around every one of my loved ones. It will move with them as they move and protect them from anything Mabuz may throw at them.

"Please keep Aria and Zoe close. Everyone is protected, but I wouldn't put it past Mabuz to use them if he can," I warn Gregor, who nods his head.

"It's fine, Glory. We will make sure they are not anywhere near him." Nolan filled his parents in on what's going to go down tonight. I can see Luc whispering to my mom and fathers while Mason fills in my siblings. My and Luc's mates know what's about to happen.

"Oh, Glory, I'm so sorry that you have to do this. It's all my fault," my mother wails dramatically, and I roll my eyes.

"Relax, Mom, I've got this." I do, I know exactly what I'm going to do.

Luc leads the way, and I follow with my mates behind me, my family following them. Our party walks down the middle aisle of the throne room toward the front dais, and I smile as I see all of the demons present sporting large, fluffy wings. I'm pretty sure the skies of Hell are going to become pretty chaotic over the next few days.

The crowd falls silent as they catch sight of the procession, and they all bow their heads, and I hear whispers of, "Hail, Glory" throughout the crowd. Luc carries the crown of Hell in front of him on a pillow, Leviathan has Lilith's sword in one hand, and Beelzebub has some kind of scepter I haven't seen before. I follow behind the three of them, and we climb the stairs, followed by my family. I turn to face the crowd and smile as I see the little girls waving regally to everyone, bringing smiles and cheers from my citizens.

"Ladies and gentlemen," Luc begins, and the crowd falls silent once more. "It has been my life-long pleasure to be your ruler from the start, but it is time for a new era, and you can already tell it's going to be one to remember. You can thank your new queen for the wings on your back. Angels will no longer be able to take our birthright from us. Glory plans to put a stop to the atrocity of cutting off an angel's wings if they are deemed too sinful for Heaven." He pauses, and the crowd roars so loudly it feels like the whole building shakes. "It is my supreme honor to crown your new queen. I couldn't have picked a better heir myself."

Luc gestures for me to take a seat on the throne. I'm sweeping my dress to the side when a commotion at the great double doors draws our attention. Striding down the carpeted walkway is Captain Jack Sparrow in a dove gray morning suit. His dreads are tied back with a velvet headband, and he has rings on every finger. He even holds his hand up the same way, a little bit effeminate. What the actual fuck? Seriously, I look around to see if I'm being pranked, but no, Luc is glaring at the man I'm assuming is Mabuz.

"Mabuz!" my mother and Ben hiss in unison, and then my eyes drift to the people following him down.

"Bridgette," Nolan growls as I watch the bane of our existence smirk at us from her place just behind Mabuz.

They come to a stop before us. Mabuz is even

carrying a sword like the fictional pirate. Now that he's closer, I can see he's not as attractive as the actor who played him in the movie. His face is pockmarked, which is weird because demons can heal most things and don't get sick. I wonder if it's a result of blood magic. Using it is rotting him inside and outside.

Chapter Eighteen

"I challenge Gloriana Luxure for the position of Hell's heir," he announces pompously, waving around his cane.

"Of course you do, so predictable," I mutter under my breath.

We all just glare at him, and his smug mien drops as he realizes he's not getting the shocked reaction he hoped for.

My mates step forward to flank me on either side as the flaming crown leaves Luc's hands and appears on my head.

"You're too late," Mason calls out, his grin wicked as he looks down at his nemesis.

"Way too late." Ben steps up next to me, and Mabuz glares at me.

"That is my demon. You need to return him to me immediately," he spits out, and I just laugh.

"You can't own demons, and he is my mate. You don't even get to look at him anymore." I see Mabuz's temper rise as his face flushes red.

"Mabuz, you are being charged with crimes against the crown, demons, and humankind. You have been sentenced to death. Do you have anything to say?" I pause, hoping he will summon the book he stole from our family.

Sure enough, his arrogance knows no bounds, and the book quickly appears in his hand. He uses his cane and slices out. To my horror, he draws it across Bridgette's neck. She screams and grabs the wound, but it's fatal, and she falls to the ground dead, her blood pooling on the floor around her as he starts chanting.

"Fuck," I hear Nolan mutter as he spreads his wings so his girls can't see what happened. I'm hoping they were back far enough that they didn't. I hear my brothers offer to take the girls away, and Levi points to an antechamber off to the side. The four of them surround the girls and usher them away with promises of sweets and treats. I see Luc wave his hand, so he must be conjuring them for my daughters, and I smile at him in thanks.

Mabuz's chanting rises in volume when he sees no one is paying attention.

"That was always the problem with those spells. They require so much faffing around," Luc tells me conversationally while I am still in shock that he killed Bridgette to fuel his spell. "Well, are you going to deal with that?" he asks and nudges me with his elbow.

It has the desired effect, and I brush off my shock and conjure an item into my hand. Pressing down on the trigger, I shoot a new and improved Sparky at the demon in front of me and watch with pleasure as a hundred thousand volts shoot through his body. He screams and convulses, dropping the book and pissing his pants before collapsing to the ground.

The crowd around us cheers while the entourage he brought with him looks on with a mixture of horror and relief. Leaving my chair, I lift my skirts and descend the stairs until I stand over him. I watch as Teddy leans down and picks up the book, his nose wrinkled with disgust. Unfortunately, it fell in the puddle of blood surrounding Bridgette. I wave a hand, so it's instantly clean, and he smiles gratefully at me. I've tasked him with looking after it for now until I can use it to reverse all the spells. He's my most solid and down-to-earth mate, and I know he won't even open it, whereas some of the others may be tempted to peek.

"You have been a very bad man," I remark conversationally to the lump of flesh still twitching beneath my feet. "Delusions of grandeur are never attractive. I'm not sure what happens to us when we die, but I hope there is a place for you where you will spend eternity burning for your crimes."

My magic takes over and lifts Mabuz into the air, where he starts to burn. It looks suspiciously like the flame of Hell from beneath Mt. Doom. There's a flash of light, and he disappears, and I know instinctively that he has been transported to that exact room to spend all of eternity burning. I'm not sure if that's a great idea, since I'd like to kill him and be done with it, but for now, that will do.

I wave a hand, and the people with him are freed from his enchantments. The demons fall to the ground, sobbing their thanks, while the humans look around, confused and dazed. Their memories will need to be wiped before they are returned to wherever they came from. I look at my uncle.

"One last task before you leave to chase down Kerry. Please take the humans with you." I gesture to them, and he bows his head.

"Thank you."

"Go now. I won't hold you back any longer."

He leans in and kisses me before gesturing to his mates for them to join him. The three of them walk down and gather the humans close to them, and in a flash of light, they disappear.

Smiling, I wonder if I should give Kerry a heads-up, but I decide not to. Truthfully, I want Luc to win and bring my friend to Hell.

I climb back up the stairs and turn to face my people. "As my first declaration, I declare motor vehicles the mode of transport in Hell once more. Those people who used to work as mechanics and garage attendants are all ordered to return to your previous jobs."

There's a loud cheer through the crowd.

"Wings and flying will also be acceptable, but please practice flying. The open plains between the portal and Mt. Doom are for this, and everyone must put in ten flight hours before they will be allowed to fly through the realm. I will have people recording your practice time and issuing you a flight license. Anyone found flying through the realm without their license will be issued a fine and have their wings clipped for thirty days. I don't want any midair disasters."

There's murmuring in the crowd in front of me, but none of it sounds negative, so I move on.

"There will also be a change to realm travel in the coming weeks, so please keep an eye out for announcements. I hope you will all be patient as I learn to be the best queen I can be for you all. Please enjoy the festivities out in the palace grounds."

I finish my speech, and the crowd cheers. I now have to head out onto the balcony and wave to the waiting demons. I turn my back and make my way up the stairs and to the balcony doors. My mates follow behind me, their love and support filling my chest.

We file out onto the balcony and step toward the railing, and I gape at the sheer volume of people on the palace grounds. A sea of bodies with wings stretches out as far as the eye can see. Big screens broadcast everything that happened inside the throne room, so all of them saw what happened to Mabuz and heard the declarations. When they see me, I wave, and they burst into applause, cheering, whistling, and shouting congratulations.

"Holy crap," I mutter to my mates out of the side of my mouth. "I had no idea there were this many demons."

"I think every single one of them returned for your coronation." Louis's hand is a steady weight on my back.

"Fuck, I hope I can do them justice. I don't want to let them down."

"Babe, I have no doubt that you are going to be one hell of a ruler." Carter presses a kiss to my shoulder.

The crowd starts to chant, and I can't help but smile. Life is never going to be boring.

"All hail Glory, may her reign be glorious."

Thank you so much for reading Glory's final book. I hope you've enjoyed the journey as much as I have. If you loved it, don't forget to leave a review, it helps it get seen by people.

In the mean time why don't you check out one of my other series. You can find everything you need to know here.

www.lexiewinston.com

As usual I have thanks to convey to the people who help produce my stories.

To my cover designer Tash of Dazed Designs I know it's a struggle working with me but we get there in the end.

Thank you to Jess at Elemental Editing. In the words of Tina Turner, you're simply the best.

Thanks to Tegan and Kerry. Beta reader extraordinaires.

And lastly to you guys the readers. I love what I do, and probably would do it regardless if anyone read them or not, but you guys make it that much sweeter so thank you.

Until next time, happy reading

Lexie